Awakened

T. Allen Madding

Awakened

T. Allen Madding

Copyright ©2017 Todd Allen Madding

Editor *Crystal Rowe*

Cover Design   *T. Allen Madding*

ISBN 978-0692926413

Library of Congress Control Number: 2017911737

This is a work of fiction. Names and characters are the product of the author's imagination. Any resemblance to actual persons, living or dead is purely coincidental. While places, cities, and events may be actual, all characters are fictitious.

.

Dedication

To my loving daughter, Lindsey Madding Adkins. You have been my biggest fan and cheerleader since the day you were born. Through some of the darkest and loneliest days in my life, you chose to stand beside me and encourage me. For that I will always be grateful. I love you with every fiber of my being.

- Daddy

Contents

"If the local church wants to be the hope of the world, it needs to step into places in which people find themselves hopeless"

Jarrid Wilson

Awakened

Chapter 1

Samuel Matthews awoke with his back aching. He slowly lifted himself to a sitting position on the edge of the sofa and retrieved his wire-rimmed glasses from the nearby shelf. The ticking clock over the study door showed 7AM. He slowly rose to his feet and shuffled to the window. The street below was silent – in stark contrast to the day before, when it was packed with cars trying to leave the city. The rising sun shone on the sheet of ice covering the sidewalk and street below. The grass bordering the sidewalk lay hidden below a few inches of snow. He stood at the window peering at the tranquil scenery for several moments, lost in his thoughts. After several minutes, he refocused his tired eyes and shuffled for the door to the hallway.

Stepping into the hallway, he slowly made his way to the educational wing that just days before sat empty and unused. He stopped at the first classroom and quietly opened the door just enough to look in upon the sleeping refugees from the bitter winter storm. Army cots lined the walls and through the center of the room. Through the dim morning light, he could make out the faint images of mothers and children huddled under wool blankets. He quietly closed the door, making every effort not to disturb the tired souls who had survived a frightful afternoon. When he found the door to the next room unlatched and partially open, he poked his head through the opening and took a peek. Another 10-12 cots filled the room along with tattered backpacks and plastic grocery bags stuffed with dirty clothing. The nearest sleeping body had a head full of tangled hair that framed a weathered face. Directly under the cot was a pair of work boots that showed signs of age and disrepair. His nose burned as he peered in the door from the musk of a dozen bodies that had not showered in what he estimated to be at least a month.

He quietly backed into the hallway, paused for a moment, and drew a breath of the cleaner air. He then proceeded to the next classroom, and then the next, repeating the process 30 more times before reaching the end of the hall that led to the gymnasium. As he rounded the corner, his nose detected a different scent - that of fresh, hot coffee. He pushed open a door and stepped into the darkened gym, carefully moving around the perimeter of the gym floor in fear of stepping on a sleeping soul lying on a thin mat. He found his way to the door to the kitchen by the dim light peeking out from under the door. As he pushed the door open and stepped into the kitchen, he squinted at the light of the room.

As his eyes adjusted from the darkened gym, he lifted his glance to see six volunteers huddled over the stoves. He recognized Phil and Alvin as he made his way towards four large coffee urns and began to fill a Styrofoam cup. Phil looked up from his work to catch the old pastor's eye.

"Morning Rev. Sam," he said.

"Good morning, Phil," Sam replied. "Did you get any sleep?"

"Yeah, we managed to put a few cots up on the stage area. I slept on and off for about 4 hours or so. Figured we'd have 500 hungry faces greeting us soon, so we started scrambling some eggs and frying some bacon and sausage."

Alvin looked up and Sam quickly realized he was wearing an apron covered in flour.

"Biscuit maker, I presume?" Sam inquired.

"You betcha!" Alvin replied with a smile.

Sam returned a tired smile and headed back to the gymnasium nursing the cup of coffee. As he stepped back into the gym, he noticed the lights were beginning to come on. The gym lights took several minutes from when they were first powered on until they were fully light. He looked across the gym to see what seemed like hundreds of mats dotting the floor – some still had sleeping bodies, some were covered in a pile of pillows, blankets, and clothing. People were walking in and out of the gym locker rooms. Some were headed for the showers, while others were walking out with toothbrushes sticking out the corner of their mouths.

The amount of supplies that had been provided by the Red Cross, the National Guard, and the Atlanta Mission staggered his mind. But there they were, hundreds of people from varied walks of life quietly living inside the church building that had lain silent for several years. He returned to the hallway where several volunteers were organizing a table by the door to meet any additional walk-ins who had weathered the night and might be seeking shelter this morning.

Sam walked back into his office and turned on his radio to catch the local news and an update on the weather. He sat motionless as he listened, occasionally taking a long sip of coffee as the news report continued.

The highways and interstates were still shut down, but State of Georgia and county employees had worked through the night sanding bridges, moving stuck tractor-trailers and clearing wrecked vehicles. The Governor's office and the Mayor's office had both released statements requesting everyone stay off the roads for 24 hours to allow crews to clear wrecked and stalled vehicles. Grocery stores reported outages of milk, bread, and water. Utility companies were reporting over 650,000 residents without power. The airport had been another shelter, with stranded travelers sleeping in concourse aisles, at airline gates, and in the main terminal. Hundreds of flights had been cancelled or delayed while crews worked to clear runways and de-ice aircraft.

As Sam listened to the news, he began to wonder. This storm had stranded a lot of office workers from the office buildings and skyscrapers around the church, but it had also proven too much to withstand for the homeless that typically slept in parks, under bridges, and in doorways around the city. But Atlanta had many freezing nights in the winter. What did those who were homeless do on those nights? The Atlanta Mission was a huge building, but it couldn't house the entire homeless community on one night. His mind went back to the man found frozen on the steps of the sanctuary just a few weeks ago. While what he had witnessed over the last 24 hours was a great and wonderful thing, it was obvious to him there was a great deal more that needed to be done. Where could he start? Where would he get the money? He removed the wire-rimmed glasses and rubbed his tired eyes.

Chapter 2

Fred opened his eyes to the burning pain in his lower back. He shuffled around on the military cot that had been his bed for the night trying to find some relief and a semblance of comfort. He reached below the cot and patted his backpack and boots. He always worried about sleeping in shelters because of the theft of his limited belongings, but hard times can sometimes cause a man to make difficult decisions that he might otherwise not choose. Last night's storm had been one of those times. He had awakened several times during the night scared someone had stolen his boots when he realized his feet were not heavy, but after a couple minutes he would realize where he was and pat the boots under his cot to comfort his mind.

As he laid in the dark staring at the ceiling, he wondered about Gladys. The military boys seemed to have been taking good care of her, but he had to wonder if she had gotten to the hospital okay. He wondered how the emergency room had treated her. Hospitals could be pretty uncompassionate towards homeless folk, he thought. And on a night as bad as this one, he wondered how packed the emergency rooms were.

Silently, he began to pray, "So yeah, um, God. Miss Gladys has had a pretty tough go of it with this storm. I know I prolly ain't in too good a standing to be asking for favors and such, but she's always seemed like good people. Please pull on the hearts of the nurses and folks over at Grady Emergency Room to have some mercy on her and help her. I know she was hurting pretty bad, and she had been in that snow for a while. Please have 'em to warm her up, do whatever surgery she needs, and make her comfortable. I won't bother you with anything else. I imagine you're pretty busy with all the folks in this storm worried about their kids and families. So I'll let you get back to all that, but please look out for Gladys. I'm pretty sure she is one of yours."

He rolled over on his side which seemed to give him a smattering of relief and tried to go back to sleep. He lay there for a few minutes and then silently began to pray again.

"Um, God, sorry to interrupt you again, but I just thought it was pretty rude to be asking a favor without saying a thank you. It sure is nice to be lying on a cot instead of on a concrete step and the heat in this building sure is nice on a night like tonight. Thank you for the folks downstairs that made all them sandwiches and soup and gave us all blankets. I don't know much about this church, but they must be pretty decent folks to let some stinking street vagrant like me sleep in their place and feed me. Anyhow. Thanks. This night is a might better than I had thought it was gonna be."

He reached under the cot, patted his backpack and boots, and settled back in to sleep.

Chapter 3

Gladys looked around the exam room and wondered what was going to happen next. She was grateful for the stack of heated blankets they had piled on her and for the pain medications they were giving her for her hip. The nurses and staff had rumbled her up and down the hall to X-Ray rooms and every kind of scan she had ever imaged and a few more. Just as she was mid-thought, in popped that little redheaded nurse that had been working with her.

"Miss Gladys," the little redhead said, "the doctor is going to be in to see you in just few minutes. We have got all your lab work, scans, and X-Rays back, so he should be able to tell you what our treatment plan is going to be. How are those pain meds working? On a scale of 1 to 10 with 10 being the worse pain you have ever experienced in your life, what would you rate your current pain?"

Gladys twitched her nose, "I'd say a solid 7."

"Well that is a definite improvement over the 10 score you gave me when they brought you in, so I'd say we're making some progress," said the little redhead.

Gladys smiled, "Yeah and I'm not shivering anymore so there's that," she replied.

"Well, Miss Gladys, if you need any more of those heated blankets, you just let me know."

Gladys closed her eyes and tried to think of something to take her mind off the pain. Her mind quickly drifted back to the office building where Starbucks and Chick-Fil-A were. She was just fine sitting there until they kicked her out in the cold. If they had left her alone, she probably would not have fallen and she wouldn't be in this blasted hospital, she thought to herself. But what is done is done. She sighed a quiet sigh and folded her hands across her abdomen.

"Dang the lights in this room are bright," Gladys thought. "If they shut the dang things off I might be able to sleep with these meds."

As she lay there quietly, she could hear the steady tick of a clock in the room.

"Yeah, that would make it hard to sleep too I imagine," she thought.

A machine to her left made a purring sound, and the cuff on her arm began to tighten. After a minute or two the cuff began to deflate and the machine beeped a couple of times.

"They sure don't want you sleeping around here," Gladys thought.

With sleep seeming to not be a ready option, Gladys began to silently pray, "God thank you for not letting me freeze to death out there on that sidewalk. Thank you for those military folk that got me out of the snow and to the hospital in that rough riding overgrown Jeep looking thing they had. Thank you for the sweet little redheaded gal that's been helping me. I can't remember her name for the life of me, but she sure is sweet and trying to take care of me best as she can. Bless whatever intern they give me to have enough sense to figure out what to do, 'cause this pain is a bit more than I can live with on a regular basis. I'm a tough ol' bat, but this is a bit much. Please bless all the other homeless folks out there on the streets tonight that they might get some shelter from this storm, and if you could find a way to let me sleep a little, I'd be mighty grateful. Amen."

Gladys lay still with her eyes closed and tried to sleep. The next thing she knew, she was hearing a voice calling her name.

"Gladys. Gladys," the voice called.

Confused for a second she tried to clear the fogginess of her mind. Who was calling her? It was a man's voice. Was it God? Had she died and the creator was now calling her name? With her eyes still closed, she tried to turn her head towards the voice.

"Gladys!" The voice called again; this time with a little more enthusiasm.

She wrinkled her brow as she tried to understand what was happening.

"Yes?" She replied faintly.

"Gladys, I am an orthopedic surgeon," said the voice. "The Emergency Room staff called me in to review your X-rays and your injuries. You have a broken hip. This is a pretty common injury for senior adults. We find the hip weakens as many adults get older, and then at some time they take a step or slip a little and the hip breaks and they fall. From reviewing your X-rays, I believe that is exactly the case with your injury. I understand you were out in the storm walking to a shelter and fell. I believe your hip gave way causing you to fall. This is a pretty straight-forward procedure. I am going to take you to surgery and insert a couple of pins in your hip to strengthen it and allow it to mend. You'll spend a week or so recovering, and we will have you up and walking around in no time. An anesthesiologist will be along shortly and will become your new best friend. She will give you a medicine in your IV that will help you relax and then we will get you to the Operating Room where she will get you to a nice peaceful sleep for the surgery. Do you have any questions or concerns?"

Gladys squinted her eyes towards the direction of the voice. How long had she slept? She continued to squint until she could make out the face of a young sandy blonde headed kid in a lab coat that did not look old enough to shave in her opinion.

"Doc," she started, "if y'all can help me sleep and ease this pain. I'd be mighty obliged," she said.

"Don't you worry Gladys. We are going to help you with both of those requests. I'll see you in a few minutes. Try to relax."

The young doctor disappeared out of her line of sight. She could hear a few voices in the distance but could not make out what they were saying. She closed her eyes again.

"Gladys," another voice soon was calling.

"That's me," she replied.

"Gladys, I am the anesthesiologist. Are you allergic to any medications?"

"Not that I know of," Gladys replied to the middle-aged lady looking over the top of a pair of glasses.

"Ever had any surgeries? Ever had any problems with any kinds of anesthesia?

"Twenty years ago I had my appendix out," Gladys answered, "But I don't remember having any problems."

"Ok. That's great," said the woman. "I'm gonna start a medication to help you relax and take some of the edge off your pain. It may even make you a little drowsy. Then once they get you into the Operating Room, I will give you another medication that will help you go into a really nice deep sleep."

"That sounds wonderful," Gladys responded, "I'm worn out and haven't been able to sleep since I fell."

The woman gently patted Gladys on the shoulder.

"Don't you worry, sweetie," she said; "We will get you some sleep very shortly."

The woman injected a medication into the IV bag hanging on the pole just to the left of Gladys shoulder. She stood silently watching Gladys and then the IV. After several minutes, she stepped back closer to the side of the bed.

"How are you doing now, Gladys?" she asked.

"Well. I'm a little foggy and kinda feel like I could sleep," Gladys replied.

"Alrighty then," the woman responded; "Don't struggle with it. Relax and get some rest."

The woman disappeared out of Gladys' sight and Gladys closed her eyes and soon fell asleep .

Chapter 4

As Sam sat in his office listening to the news, a thought popped into his head. A homeless man had been brought in last night talking about a homeless lady that he had found lying covered in snow as he was making his way to their shelter. His mind began to process the situation. The man had told him that she was a lady he regularly encountered, so Sam knew there would be no family or friends checking on her. She would be just another face being processed through Grady's Emergency and Surgery Centers. If her hip was broken as the man had seemed to believe, she would be in the hospital for a couple of weeks and then would need therapy to return to walking. He knew this was a pretty painful recovery for an elderly person as he had visited several of his flock who had been through the procedure and recovery. The fact she was homeless added to the difficulties that lie ahead for her. Where would she convalesce after being released from the hospital? How would she get to follow-up appointments?

All of the big picture things that had burdened Sam's mind several minutes ago were now completely out of his mind. He needed to find this woman and be the family for her that she currently did not have. Fortunately for him, he was on the pastoral care team at Grady and received a daily listing of patients who sought clergy. But if she did not check that box on the admitting paperwork, she would not be in the email he received every morning. Sam was very familiar with the Health Insurance Portability and Accountability Act (HIPAA) and the protection of patient privacy, so he knew it might take some maneuvering for him to locate her and assist her. But Sam was determined. He needed to locate the homeless guy from the night before and get a few details.

With the sound of some popping and cracking in his joints, Sam stood up from his desk and headed to the fellowship hall. He knew breakfast was cooking and the people sheltered in his church would begin to trickle in to eat.

When he walked into the fellowship hall, it was alive with commotion. There was already a line of approximately 100 people waiting for a plate of breakfast. The smell of eggs and bacon filled the air, and his old nose caught the delightful aroma of coffee. He smiled and made his way towards two tables hosting a dozen insulated containers of coffee with the words "U.S. National Guard" stenciled on the side. He filled another styrofoam cup with the hot nectar and bypassed the sugar and creamer containers. Black coffee had been a constant source of comfort and strength years ago in college and seminary for him, and now he never gave sugar or creamer a second thought.

As he drew his first sip from the steaming cup, he noticed a couple of the Guardsman standing near the door to the alley. He walked to them and greeted them.

"Good Morning," he started.

Two young men and a young woman he estimated to be in their mid 20s looked up and smiled.

"Good Morning, Pastor," one replied, "How are you this brisk morning?"

Sam smiled, "I can't complain. And who would want to listen to it if I did?!"

The three chuckled.

"Pretty brutal night last night," said the young lady. "These folks are really appreciative that you opened the church to provide them shelter."

"Glad we could help," Sam said. "I have a question for you. One of the homeless guys I spoke with last night was telling me he had discovered a lady covered in snow last night. Did any of you hear anything about her?"

The Guardsman on the end looked up quickly.

"Yes, Sir," he responded. "Gladys. Her name is Gladys. She had a broken hip and had fallen and lost consciousness. My squad transported her to Grady ER last night."

Sam smiled again, "I wanted to visit her and see if I could help her in any way. Knowing she is homeless, I know she won't have a family to lean on for help."

"Let me get my squad leader for you, Sir," the young Guardsman replied.

He quickly disappeared out the door. After a few minutes, he walked back in the door with a Captain in tow.

"Captain Miller, this is the Pastor of this church. He was hoping to visit the homeless lady we transported to the ER last night with the broken hip," the young Guardsman said.

Captain Miller extended his hand and shook hands with Sam.

"Samuel Matthews, Sir," Sam said as he shook the Captain's hand.

"Good to meet you, Pastor," the Captain responded. "Since the lady had no next of kin for us to notify, I sat at the hospital until about an hour ago. They were taking her to surgery when I left."

"Do you think you could get me over there in the mess the streets are today?" Sam asked.

"Without a doubt, Sir," the Captain said; "My squad has been maneuvering the city pretty well."

"Corporal," the Captain called to one of the Guardsman, "The pastor and I need transportation to Grady."

"Yes, Sir," the young lady replied, "I will ready a Hummer."

She scrambled out the door. Within a few minutes she reappeared and walked directly to them.

"Pastor," it is still pretty cold outside. You probably ought to put on this parka," she said handing him a heavy dark green parka with a fur lined hood.

"And here are a pair of our arctic mittens," she said as she handed him the gloves.

Sam pulled the heavy parka on and then the mittens. He looked at the odd gloves without individual fingers in amazement. He had never worn any gloves so thick in his life. The Corporal escorted Sam and the Captain to a Hummer waiting just outside the door. He pulled himself up into the giant truck and settled into a seat.

"Buckle up Pastor," said the Captain; "This will be a bumpy ride avoiding stalled cars and other obstacles."

Sam quietly complied, pulling on a seat belt and buckling it around himself. The Hummer proceeded down the street and at the first intersection he saw four or five cars blocking the street. Without a word, the driver jumped the curb with one set of wheels and maneuvered around the mess. They proceeded down the street jumping the curb on a frequent basis. Sam was shocked at the number of abandoned and wrecked cars they encountered on the way. He had made the drive to Grady so many times over the years, he had hardly paid any attention to landmarks and sites along the way. But today, maneuvering the streets was so difficult, they were traveling around 15 miles an hour. Everything was going by so slowly, so the old pastor had a great deal of time to look at everything along the way. Everything was covered in snow or a layer of ice. Tree limbs bowed under the weight of the ice and occasionally, he would hear a loud crack when a limb would snap under the weight of the ice. It was an eerie experience for Sam. Normally, he would encounter a great deal of traffic along the route and would see numerous pedestrians. But today, the city seemed lifeless. He saw no other cars moving on the streets. There were no pedestrians on the sidewalks. It was almost depressing to see the empty streets and abandoned cars.

The short trip took the group an hour to complete. When they arrived at Grady Hospital, Sam noticed a change in its normal appearance. The

Emergency Ambulance entrance was double stacked with ambulances and military Hummers. He could see a dozen or so people wrapped in parkas pushing stretchers into the Emergency entrance.

When the Hummer pulled up to the main Emergency entrance, a Guardsman rushed to the rear door of the Hummer and assisted Sam and the Captain exiting the vehicle.

"Watch your step, Sirs," the young Guardsman said; "We have been salting the drive and sidewalk, but ice is continuing to form."

They made their way into the Emergency Entrance, and Sam could see approximately 50 people in the waiting room. He unzipped the heavy parka and retrieved his Clergy identification badge from his coat pocket. He signed in as he had done a hundred times before and picked up the clipboard marked "Patients seeking clergy." He scanned the list but did not see any listing that he thought would be Gladys. He looked at the Captain.

"I don't see her on the visitation list," Sam said.

The Captain looked up and grinned. "She signed me in as her legal guardian, so I can get you in to see her."

The Captain had a brief discussion at the admitting desk and then pointed to the hallway door.

"She went to surgery two hours ago, so we have to go up to the surgery Center," he reported.

As they made their way down the hallway towards the elevators, Sam held up his hand. He punched a code into a door lock and opened the door to reveal a small kitchenette.

"Coffee, Captain?"

"Absolutely!"

Sam poured two cups of coffee, handed one to the Captain, and then proceeded down the hallway.

When they reached the elevator, Sam instinctually punched the up button. When the elevator doors opened, a middle aged redheaded nurse stepped out and smiled a huge smile.

"Pastor Sam!" She exclaimed excitedly, giving him a huge hug. "So good to see you!"

Sam smiled and looked at the Captain, "Perks of the job," he said jokingly.

They stepped into the elevator car and, without giving it much thought, Sam punched the button for the 5th floor. He had been to the Surgery Suite so many times it was almost automatic. When they stepped off the elevator, he led them directly to the patient advisory desk. The man behind the desk looked up and recognized the Captain.

"Hey, you made it back," he said seeming surprised. "They completed the surgery and she is in the Recovery Room now. You should be able to see her in a few minutes."

The two men found a couple open seats in the Surgery Waiting area and quietly sipped their coffees. Sam began thinking of how Peachtree Church could continue to minister to the families they had sheltered during this storm after things resumed to normal. He wondered how they would pay the power bill after heating the Education Wing for more than just enough to keep pipes from freezing for the first time in 5 years. Granted there were many people sheltered at the church who had homes to return to after the roads cleared, but there were many that were homeless when they walked in the door and would return to homelessness.

It was a complex problem that could not be solved by handing out one meal or providing one sleeping bag. There were numerous situations that resulted in each homeless persons journey. How could those paths be altered? Sam had been around the streets of Atlanta long enough. He knew it was not a problem that could be solved overnight. And it would not be solved by the next person to win the Mayor's race. Many had tried over the years with various initiatives, but the problem remained.

Sam looked around the waiting area for something to distract his thoughts. As his eyes surveyed the room, he saw a magazine rack on the wall. He walked over and perused the collection – most of which was at least 6 months out of date. He shook his head and returned to his seat.

"So Captain," he said, "what part of the area do you live?"

The Captain raised his head and replied, "Down near the Speedway."

Sam looked confused.

The Captain recognized the look and quickly attempted to clarify; "Atlanta Motor Speedway. Hampton."

"Oh," Sam replied. "And what do you do fulltime?"

"Well I am going to college and working security at the Atlanta Airport," the Captain answered. "It keeps you busy balancing all of the time commitments, but I have my goals in sight."

"Do you have a lot of homeless in the Hampton area?" Sam inquired.

"Some," the Captain replied; "But a drop in the bucket to what you guys have in the inner city. How do you address such a large homeless community?"

Sam shook his head, "Many have tried different programs and such, but the problem has not been effectively addressed. I am sitting here trying to figure out the answer myself. When we opened the church doors for the storm, I expected we would see lots of stranded commuters and a handful of homeless. But what I noticed last night and this morning walking the halls is that we really saw a mix of demographics and a lot more homeless than I expected. I really think it is a huge need and the Church as a whole should be actively seeking to serve and solve the need. But our struggle is that our Church has withered and barely pays the light bill. In fact, this is the first time in over five years that we have had anyone in the education wing, gym and fellowship hall. The more I think about it, it is almost like as a church, we have fallen into serving ourselves and maintaining instead of servicing the community."

The Captain nodded.

"That's a shame," he said. "That's a really nice facility y'all have there and it's in a prominent location."

"Expensive real estate is what it is," Sam responded; "and expensive to maintain and operate."

"I always wondered if the homeless in the city would be willing to locate to another area of the town if they had a comfortable place to live. You know some kind of community," the Captain said.

A lady sitting to the right of the Captain suddenly spoke up, "Sorry to eavesdrop on your conversation. But I couldn't help but hear your discussion. "

Both men looked up at a short grey haired lady that Sam guessed was 65 or more.

"I have a son-in-law that lives in Austin, Texas, and he was telling me about an organization he volunteers with out there. For years they ran food trucks delivering food to homeless and struggling families. About a year or so ago, they started a master planned community just outside Austin for the homeless. They have old restored travel trailers and tiny houses where each person has a clean, comfortable, safe place to live. They have doctors and counselors who volunteer there at an onsite community clinic, and they provide job training. I bet something like that would work in a city like Atlanta. You would just have to find a big enough plot of land to house it."

Sam felt a chill run down his spine as the woman talked.

"What is the name of the organization?" he asked.

"Mobile Loaves and Fishes," she replied.

Sam pulled out his notebook and jotted down the name.

"I'm going to have to research that one," he said with a smile.

After a few more quiet minutes, the man from the desk approached them.

"Captain," he started, "Miss Boatwright is ready to be moved to a room."

The Captain looked confused.

"Miss Boatwright, um, Gladys?" the man responded.

"Oh!" The Captain exclaimed. "Don't know that I have heard her last name until now."

"If you gentlemen will follow me, I will take you over to meet her on the way."

They proceeded thru a set of double doors, down a corridor and around a corner where they met an orderly pushing a hospital bed out of another room.

"Josh," the man said, "This is the family for Miss Boatwright."

The orderly looked up at the two men and then down at the patient and then looked back up a bit bewildered.

"Not natural family," said the Captain.

"Community family," interjected Sam.

"Ah. OK." The orderly responded, "Hi. I'm Josh. She seems to being doing well. She's a little bit groggy but surgery went well, and she has not had any complications in recovery."

Chapter 5

Alvin sat quietly in the kitchen at the end of the large prep table eating a plate of breakfast and revisiting the events of the last 24 hours in his mind. Peachtree Church had sheltered some 500 people over the night. That was more people than the church had under its roof in any one month over the last year. He figured that at least 200 of them were homeless. He then began calculating numbers in his head. If 45 shelters opened in the city, and they each sheltered around 200 people, and a third of those were homeless, then that would mean around 3,000 homeless had been sheltered over the night. He shook his head at the thought. That was the equivalent of a small town. How could a community that size be adequately served? Not just housed and fed - but served? How could an organization meet medical needs, counseling needs, drug and or alcohol rehabilitation needs, and physical therapy needs? How could a ministry provide job placement services, resume writing services, and job training for a community that size? It seemed overwhelming.

As he ate the plate of food, he remembered a video he had watched several months back of Andy Stanley, the son of First Baptist pastor, Charles Stanley. He could not recall Andy's whole message, but he remembered one phrase that had caught his attention, "Do for one what you wish you could do for all".

"OK," Alvin said to seemingly no one; "So what could I do for one?"

Alvin gave the question careful consideration. His work at the GM plant was not a direct skill that would be marketable anymore with the closing of assembly plants and such.

"What is it that I have to offer?"

As he sat sorting through the questions running through his mind, he heard a rustling noise that demanded his attention. He adjusted his focus to see that Phil had walked into the kitchen and was putting serving trays into the sink.

Alvin thought for a second and then spoke up.

"Phil, we have worked almost 24 hours now. Reckon some of the folks out there would be willing to lend a hand with some of this cleanup?"

Phil paused and lifted an eyebrow.

"You know, I hadn't even thought of that," Phil said; "But I am a bit tired. Maybe it wouldn't hurt to ask."

Alvin wiped his hands on the apron he was still wearing and walked out into the fellowship hall. He stepped into the center of the room and in a loud voice asked, "Excuse me folks, but would anyone be willing to volunteer to wash a few dishes?"

A couple of hands went up and two people approached him.

"I'd be more than glad to help wash some dishes," the first man said.

"Great," said Alvin.

He extended his hand to the man and shook his hand.

"I'm Alvin. What's your name?"

"Howdy Mister Alvin," the man replied. "My name is Fred."

A second man standing next to Fred spoke up.

"Mister Alvin," he said; "My name is Jose. Y'all have been mighty generous with the food and shelter. I'd be more than glad to help out with those dishes."

Alvin shook the man's hand and said, "Thank you, buddy. I really appreciate the help."

He led the two men back into the kitchen where Phil was scrubbing a large pot.

"Phil," he said, "I've brought in reinforcements."

Phil looked up and smiled.

"Alrighty! Thank you gentlemen for your help."

"No problem," Fred said; "I have a few years experience at this task."

Fred and Jose began washing, rinsing, and drying pots, pans, and serving trays. So Phil walked back out into the fellowship hall to check on what else needed to be done. He was surprised to see people he did not know bagging up garbage, wiping down tables, and sweeping the floor. Alvin was a few steps behind him and stopped when he noticed the same thing. Several of the National Guardsman were assisting with the cleanup work.

Alvin looked at Phil, "Let's go see what needs attention in the Educational wing," he suggested.

Phil nodded and the two headed down the hall passing more people carrying out large bags of garbage. When they arrived to the first classroom, Alvin opened the door to see an elderly lady folding a blanket. The room was spotless.

"Anything we can do to help?" Phil asked.

"No, thank you," she said with a smile, "I believe I have this under control. A little slow, maybe, but under control."

The two men walked to the next classroom and saw a young mother putting socks on a little girl while her little brother sat on the floor holding a sock.

Alvin knelt down.

"Son, can I help you with that?"

"Oh! Thank you," said the mother.

The little boy looked up at Alvin for a moment and then cautiously handed them the sock.

"Here we go," Alvin said as he helped the boy with the socks and then a pair of tennis shoes. "Looky there all laced up and ready to go!"

The little boy giggled and pushed himself up from the floor.

Alvin laughed and started to push himself up from the floor much slower than the little boy had done. Phil stepped over to him.

"How about a hand?" he said, offering Alvin assistance.

Alvin took his hand and Phil helped him to his feet.

"Not as easy as it once was," Alvin noted.

"Tell me about it," Phil replied; "Tell me about it."

Phil and Alvin continued moving down the hall room by room. Some rooms they found empty. Other rooms they found needing a little clean up. By the time they had proceeded through all the rooms on all three floors, it was almost lunchtime. They hustled back to the kitchen to prepare whatever was on hand for lunch.

When they arrived back in the fellowship hall, Phil quickly noticed there was a significantly smaller crowd than was there earlier when they were cleaning up from breakfast.

"The weather must be improving," Phil noted.

Alvin stopped and opened an exit door, and stepped outside. It was still very cold but some of the ice on the sidewalk had melted from the salt that had been spread on it. He stepped out and noted that the street alongside the church was still covered in snow. But at the intersection just ahead, he could see that Peachtree Street appeared to have been cleared. He returned to the fellowship hall to find Phil chatting with Fred who had volunteered to wash dishes earlier. Alvin noted Fred had a heavy backpack leaned against his leg.

"Well the side streets are still covered, but Peachtree looks like they have at least cleared one lane from what I could see," Alvin reported to the two men.

"Yeah," Phil replied, "Fred is contemplating heading out."

"What?" Alvin asked. "You've got to be kidding. You've got about four and a half hours of sunlight and then it's gonna be miserable."

Fred shrugged, "I figure the regular spots will be back open, and I don't wanna be a burden."

"Nonsense!" Alvin said; "Plus, we need your help with lunch prep."

Fred cocked his eyebrow. "Well, if you need some help I reckon I could hang around a bit longer."

The three men walked to the kitchen where two men and four ladies were gathered around the prep table.

"What are we working on, folks?" Alvin asked.

"We're making four different kinds of sandwiches," one lady responded. "Peanut butter and jelly, ham sandwiches with mayo, turkey sandwiches with sliced cheese, and bologna sandwiches with mustard."

"Alright," said Fred; "let me wash up, then I'll help."

The three men washed and dried their hands, donned serving gloves and joined the crew making sandwiches. By the time they had a serving tray of each kind of sandwiches ready, a line was forming in the fellowship hall.

Alvin carried a tray out to the serving line to see around 150 people still in the shelter ready to eat. Like Fred, many of the homeless had already headed out to return to their normal day-to-day life. Several stranded commuters had left to find their cars and find a way home. Alvin thought it was prudent for those who had stayed for lunch to stay the night. After setting the tray down on the serving table, he stepped toward the center of the room.

"Folks," he said in a loud voice; "The weather is still pretty rough out there and most of the roads are still a mess. We will be open for anyone wanting to stay another night in the warm. Let's bless this meal so y'all can eat."

The room got extremely quiet as Alvin bowed his head.

He began to pray, "Lord, please bless this meal to nourish our bodies. Bless everyone here and their families and keep them all safe. Thank you for this meal and for a warm place to sleep. Amen."

As the people began to go through the line, it occurred to him that he had never prayed in front of a crowd this size. It kind of startled him when he realized it. He looked around and then returned to the kitchen.

"I'd say there's probably 150 or so out there," Alvin told the kitchen crew. "I told them we'd have a place for all of them to sleep another night."

Phil looked at Fred.

"Well, guess we will be needing some help with dinner tonight and breakfast again."

Fred looked directly at Phil but gave no response. He continued preparing sandwiches silently.

Alvin looked over at Fred, "What about it Fred?" Alvin said, "You up for hanging out with us one more day? We sure could use your help."

Fred looked up at Alvin.

"Sure," he said.

Fred was not sure what to make of the current situation. In the last 10 years living on the streets of Atlanta, no one had expected anything out of him. He had not been asked to help with anything, and he certainly had not been included in anything. But now here he was helping out in this emergency shelter. He could not quite put his finger on why, but he kind of liked it. He did not mind the work. He had been used to hard work growing up and in the military, and this paled in comparison to any of that kind of labor. The more he thought about it, the part he liked the most was he could see other people benefiting from what he was doing. And heck, he had always preferred to make his own way and earn his keep over just being handed things. That had been the hardest part of being homeless for him. Adjusting to having to swallow his pride as a man and accept the charity of strangers.

Besides, no one had bothered his backpack or boots during the night. This was a different crowd than the regular shelters he had experienced. There was something different about the people that were serving here. Heck he could not remember anyone sitting down and just having a conversation with him in other shelters. In the last 24 hours, four or five of the people volunteering here had sat down next to him and just chit chatted. Yeah, he would stick around tonight and in the morning. Not having to seek shelter from the cold was a fringe benefit the way he saw it - icing on the cupcake.

Chapter 6

Joy Davidson looked around the classroom where she had slept the night before and tried to tidy things up. When she was satisfied that the room looked as good as it did when she walked into it the night before, she pulled on her coat and gloves and stepped out into the hallway. An older lady with a cheerful grin greeted her just outside the classroom door.

"Good Morning, Sugar," the lady said; "Did you sleep well?"

"Yes," Joy replied. "It took a bit for me to shut my mind down and finally go to sleep thinking about my children sleeping in their school gym, but once I got to sleep, I slept well. Thank you."

The lady smiled and nodded, "I'm so glad, dear. We are serving breakfast and coffee down in the fellowship hall. Head on down there and get a bite to eat before you try to head out."

Joy paused. She felt a sense of urgency to get out. She needed to get gas in her car and had to find roads that were open so she could get to her children's school. Who knew if she could get to that side of town or if you could get up the hill to the school, and she was not going to sit idly by wondering. But considering the conditions of the roads, she was sure if she could get to the school, it was going to take more than the usual 30-40 minutes. It might be a good idea to get something to eat before setting out on this trek.

"I guess that isn't a bad idea," she finally said.

Joy pulled her gloves off and stuffed them into the pockets of her jacket.

The lady smiled, "Well, I have always said breakfast is the most important meal of the day."

Joy laughed, "I tell my kids that all the time!"

Joy walked down three flights of stairs to the hallway that led to the fellowship hall. Three-quarters of the floor was covered in cots like she had slept on, and one corner had rows of tables and chairs. A line of tables just beyond them made a serving line where she could see 50 or so people lined up filling plates. She looked at her cellphone to see what time it was, but it was dead. She walked to the end of the line and waited her turn to get a plate. The smell of eggs and bacon mixed with brewed coffee reminded her of her grandmother's kitchen when she was younger. Just the memory put her in a good mood.

Joy fixed a plate of breakfast, got a cup of coffee and stirred in some creamer and a couple packets of sugar. She then found a table with an available seat and sat down to eat. She closed her eyes and quietly bowed her head and offered up a silent prayer.

"Jesus thank you for a warm place to sleep on a miserable night and the kindness of strangers to help me find this shelter. Thank you for this warm plate of food. Thank you for keeping Cheryl and Jeremy safe and warm at their school. Thank you for the teachers at the school who spent the night looking out for them. Please make a way for me to get the car running and a path for me to get to the school and get them home. Amen."

When she opened her eyes, she picked up a plastic fork and scooped a serving of eggs. When she lifted her eyes, she saw a smiling face across from her, a young woman in military fatigues sipping a cup of coffee.

"Good Morning," the young woman greeted her. "I'm Beth. How are you this morning?"

Joy smiled, "I'm doing well. I'm Joy. Nice to meet you, Beth."

Joy began eating and Beth continued the conversation, "So were you one of the folks stranded out on I-75 last night?"

Joy shook her head, "I work on the other side of the interstate. The ramps were backed up, and I started running out of gas sitting. So, I came across the bridge to a gas station on Spring Street, but it was closed. I ran out of gas before I could find another station."

35

"Well that sucks," Beth replied.

Joy nodded, "Yeah, I was trying to go pick my kids up from school, but never made it."

"Where's your car?"

Joy swallowed a fork of food and said, "The corner of 14th and Peachtree. Right in front of Colony Square."

Beth nodded and said, "just down the street a couple blocks here. Alright. Let me see if we can't help you with that. Finish your breakfast, and I'll talk to my PL."

Beth pushed herself back from the table, collected her plate and utensils and carried them to a nearby trashcan. She walked to the corner of the room by an outside door and spoke with a small group of men and women in military uniforms. After a few minutes, she walked back over where Joy was sitting. Joy had finished eating and was picking up her napkin, utensils and Styrofoam plate to toss in the trash when Beth walked up.

"Good news, Joy!" Then she giggled; "Or should I say Behold! I bring glad tidings of Joy!"

Joy laughed.

"We have a couple of four wheeler ATVs, jerry jugs of gas and battery jump boxes sitting outside ready to go," Beth reported. "If you think you are up for a ride, I'll take you to your car and see if we can't get you moving to check on your children."

Joy dropped everything in her hands on the table and gave Beth a huge hug.

"That's Awesome!" she squealed.

Joy caught herself, stepped back and looked a bit sheepish.

"Oh sorry. Are you going to get into trouble for a civilian hugging you?"

Beth laughed, "No, no. I think we're good," she laughed.

Joy picked up the trash she had dropped on the table and threw it in a trash can near the kitchen. She zipped up her coat, pulled on her gloves and looked at Beth.

"Ok," she said, "Let's get off on this adventure."

Beth led her outside where four ATVs set parked on the sidewalk and three young men in military parkas stood by.

"Sgt. Smith," Beth said, "This lady needs help getting a car started at 14th and Peachtree. She says she ran out of gas there last night."

Sgt. Smith looked up at the two, "Do you want a couple of us to go with you?" he asked as Beth pulled on a heavy parka.

"No Sergeant," she replied, "I've got this."

"Roger that," he responded; "If you have any problems, hit us up on the radio, and I'll send the Calvary."

"Will do," Beth replied.

Beth threw a leg over the nearest ATV, turned the key and pushed the starter button. The ATV roared to life almost instantly.

"Hop on, Joy," she said; "I promise not to give you a rough ride."

Joy carefully crawled on the ATV behind Beth.

"Wow, this thing is kinda roomy," she noted.

"Yeah," Beth said,; "On both sides of you there are hand holds. See 'em?"

"Yep," Joy said. "Ready to roll."

Beth pushed down on the shifter with her foot and rolled in the throttle grip with a turn of her wrist. The two eased off the curb and onto the frozen side street. They eased their way up to the corner of Peachtree where Joy could see several military vehicles parked in a line along the curb. Peachtree Street appeared to have been cleared at some point overnight. There was still snow against the curbs and small piles in the center lane, but the street looked maneuverable. Beth eased the machine North on Peachtree where there were half a dozen cars sitting motionless in the far lane.

Beth turned her head where Joy could hear her and shouted, "Which one is yours?"

Joy leaned forward and shouted back, "See that Honda up at the intersection?"

Beth replied, "Gotcha."

She drove to the rear of Joy's car and activated the four-way flashers on the ATV.

"Joy," she said, "We are in a dangerous position with cars coming down the street on 14th and Peachtree. So I am going to need you to watch out for me while I get some gas in your car. If a car starts sliding towards us or something, you holler and get to the sidewalk."

Joy replied. "Gotcha!"

Beth unstrapped a jerry jug from the ATV and a funnel and walked to the rear of the car slowly looking every direction for oncoming cars. When she was confident it was safe, She flipped open the fuel door on the side of the Honda, unscrewed the gas cap, stuck the funnel in, and removed the cap on the jerry jug. She hoisted the jug up to the funnel and began pouring gas into the car.

"Car coming," Joy called out.

Beth looked up to see a car coming South on Peachtree. It changed lanes to go around them, slowed and went by without incident. Beth watched as she continued to slowly pour gas into Joy's car. Beth patiently continued until she had as much gas in the car as she could coax out of the jug.

"OK, Joy," she said; "See if the tired old girl will crank."

Joy unlocked the door and tugged. The door was frozen shut. She gave it a hard tug - nothing. She gave it another hard tug - no movement. She gave it one more hard tug and the door opened to the sound of breaking ice. She crawled into the seat, put her key in the ignition and turned the key. All the lights on the dash came on. She waited for a couple of minutes for the fuel pump to pump gas back up to the engine and then gave it a crank. The motor turned over but did not fire. She released it and waited another minute and tried again. Again the motor turned over but did not fire. She released it and waiting again. Once again, she twisted the key, this time the motor sputtered a few times and then it started.

"Yes!" Joy exclaimed.

She reached in the floor and grabbed her ice scraper and crawled back out of the car. When she looked up, Beth had secured the jerry jug and funnel back on the ATV and was walking back with a small whisk broom. While Joy scraped at the windshield, Beth swept snow off the hood, side windows, and rear window. As the Honda started to get warmed up, the defroster began to make Joy's work a little easier.

"Ok, Joy," Beth said, "Sarge said the gas station North of here on Peachtree is open this morning. Do you have enough money to fill it up?"

Joy finished scraping off the windshield. "Yes. I sure do. I think I am good to go here. Thank you so much for all you have done to help me."

"No problem! A service of the National Guard!"

Joy crawled in the Honda and buckled her seat belt. Beth crawled on the ATV, kicked it into neutral and started it. She stood on the foot pegs of the ATV looking all directions for traffic. She motioned for Joy to go ahead. Joy put the car in drive and made a U-turn in the middle of Peachtree to head North.

"You'd never do that on a normal day in Atlanta," she thought to herself.

Beth stood motionless until Joy was headed out of sight heading North to the gas station. She then sat down on the ATV, put it in gear and headed back to the church.

When Beth arrived back at Peachtree Church, she stopped behind the row of military trucks and unstrapped the empty jerry jug. She loaded it into the first truck on the left side of the bed, and then retrieved a full jug from the right side. She strapped the jug onto the ATV and then drove back to the curb where the ATVs had been parked earlier. As she parked it, she noticed the other three ATVs were gone, as were the other squad members.

"Gonna be a long day of gassing cars today," she thought to herself.

She walked back into the warm fellowship hall to thaw out and grab a cup of coffee.

Less than five miles away, Joy was slowly making her way up Peachtree Street. Her commute was 25 miles each way. A trip that typically took 30-45 minutes depending on when she left in the mornings or afternoons that could stretch to an hour and a half if she hit rush hour today with the interstates shutdown was probably going to be over two hours. As she rounded a curve in the street, she saw the gas station on the right that Beth had told her was open. Sure enough the lights were all on, and she could see a Jeep sitting at one of the pumps. She carefully pulled into an available pump and got out to fill the car.

As Joy filled the tank on the old Honda, she watched the occasional cars go by on Peachtree Street.

"Boy, I wish traffic was this light on normal days around here," she said to herself.

As soon as the nozzle on the gas pump hose clicked off, Joy quickly put the nozzle back in the side of the pump, got the receipt from the pump, and hurried back to the warmth of the car. It was not a day to causally stand around outside. She cranked the car and prepared herself for what she expected might be a two to three hour drive. She navigated her way North on Peachtree until she reached the ramp for Highway 13 which ran parallel to the interstate, hoping the highway was open and maneuverable. As the ramp descended to the highway, she could see that the right lane had been completely cleared and about one-half of the left lane was cleared. As she began driving North on the highway, she began to pass abandoned cars on the right shoulder of the roadway. A little bit further and there was an abandoned bus on the left side partially sitting in the left lane of the highway. After about a mile she could see a pickup in front of her. She slowed her speed and maintained about a four car gap behind the truck. Normally anything more than a car and a half gap in Atlanta traffic would have someone trying to pass. But today, it seemed that everyone out on the road had opted to exercise caution, and Joy was good with that approach.

Joy looked down at the speedometer and chuckled. "30 miles an hour," she said out loud. "I can't remember the last time I drove 30 miles an hour on this highway when there wasn't a traffic jam."

Almost 30 minutes later, Joy could see where the highway crossed under I-285. She looked up as she approached the area and was shocked to see what looked like a wall of tractor-trailer rigs in both directions as far as she could see sitting stationary on the interstate. As she passed under the interstate, she slowed for abandoned vehicles on both sides of the roadway leaving a narrow path just big enough for her to maneuver. A mile or two later, she noticed the truck in front of her slowing. She moved the car a little to the left to get a look around the truck to see what was ahead of them. She could see five or six more cars in front of them. They crept along at a slower pace, and at one point there was enough of a hill that Joy could see about eight cars in front of her was a large yellow dump truck with flashing yellow lights.

"Snow plow and salt spread truck," Joy guessed out loud. "At least I will have a freshly cleared route home," she said, staying positive.

Another 30 minutes went by as they crept along until they came to the intersection for Jimmy Carter Boulevard. The traffic light separated the line of cars behind the plow. When Joy crossed the intersection, the plow was long out of her sight. She drove along still amazed by the amount of snow on the sides of the roadway and by the amount of abandoned cars on the shoulder and the occasional car that had slid off into a ditch.

When Joy began to see she was approaching Pleasant Hill Road, she was almost certain she had been driving for over an hour and a half. She carefully turned off the highway on to the road and headed for her children's school. Another 20 minutes went by as she slowly made her way to the school and to the base of the long hill that had prevented the buses reaching the school just yesterday. Joy stopped the Honda at the bottom of the hill and looked up the roadway. The road was not plowed, but she could see a set of tire tracks leading up the hill that appeared to be all the way through the layer of snow. She figured that if the tire tracks had worn down to the pavement, the Honda should have enough traction to get up the hill. She looked to both sides at the snow filled ditches. A Lexus sat at the bottom of the ditch on one side, a Dodge Minivan set halfway down towards the ditch on the other side. Those two abandoned cars did not boost her confidence, but she was determined to reach her children. She rationalized that a little head of steam would help her climb the hill, so she got a little speed up before starting the incline. The old Honda started up the hill. Joy had both hands tightly gripping the wheel. She reminded herself that the brake pedal would not be an option, so she regulated all of her speed solely with the gas pedal. Every time the car wiggled a bit, she would lightly lift off the throttle but not completely. After a few more nervous minutes, Joy reached the top of the hill and turned into the driveway of the school. As she cautiously made her way along the driveway to the Gym, she could see a handful of SUVs, pickup trucks, and Jeeps lined along the sidewalk along the Gym. As she looked at the line of parked cars, she made a startling discovery. There were no other cars around the Gym - just SUVs, pickup trucks, and Jeeps. There had been several cars sitting in the teachers' parking lot, but there were none surrounding the Gym. Apparently none of the parents had thought it safe to brave that icy hill in anything that was not four-wheel drive. As she parked her car along the sidewalk around the Gym, Joy chuckled as she thought about what she had just done.

Chapter 7

Gladys struggled to open her eyes. Her vision was blurry, and she couldn't seem to make her eyes focus. She moved her head around a little and tried opening her eyes again but things were still blurry and the light hurt her eyes. So, she closed her eyes and elected to try to sleep a bit more.

"Gladys," said a voice.

Gladys wrinkled her brow and tried to place the voice, but for the life of her she couldn't recognize it.

"Gladys," the voice called again.

"Yes?" she answered feebly.

She felt a hand pat the top of her left hand.

"Gladys, I am Reverend Samuel Matthews from Peachtree Street Church. I came to check on you and see how you were doing after your surgery to repair your broken hip."

"Oh," she replied, "Well that's mighty kind of you pastor. I've kinda been on my own for the last few years, so it's a nice surprise to have someone checking on me. Do you work for the hospital?"

"No," Sam said, "Some of the folks that found you spent the night at our church last night and told me your story. I live by myself and couldn't imagine waking from surgery with no one to be around to help care for me. These hospitals can get pretty lonely at times."

Gladys turned her head towards his voice and squinted her eyes. She could make out a fuzzy image of a grey haired man with wire-rimmed glasses.

"Pastor, I sure appreciate you coming out in this weather to check on my tired old soul. I don't know what's gonna happen with me now."

"Don't you fret, Gladys," Sam said. "You have become a defacto member of our community, and I am going to see to it you have company and help through the recovery process. The Captain of the National Guard unit that transported you here last night has been keeping a pretty good watch on you and was nice enough to drive me over in one of their huge four wheel drive vehicles."

Gladys managed a slight smile, "Those military folk sure were nice getting me out of that snow and to the hospital. That one young fella was barking orders about how to splint my leg, how to get me on a stretcher, and all. Honestly, I remember falling and being in a world of pain. The funny part about it was I felt the pain and then started falling. It seemed backwards. I hit my head hard on the way down and passed out. I came back to, and I couldn't get back up to save my life. Literally! I thought to myself if I didn't get back up that I'd freeze to death right there. But I couldn't manage to get up. I remember getting really cold and closing my eyes. I don't mean to get all out of body experience sappy, but I made my peace with God and closed my eyes. When I woke to someone calling my name, I figured it was Saint Peter, but it was Fred. My head was aching like I had been hit with a bat, and my hip was screaming. So I figured this was definitely not Heaven."

A male nurse walked into the room and began checking her vital signs.

"Miss Gladys," he said; "How we doing?"

Gladys turned her head towards his voice, squinted her eyes and replied, "I'm guessing you are doing a bit better than I am, but I'd say I'm a sight better than laying out there on that sidewalk."

The nurse chuckled.

"Alright, well we are gonna move you to a room where you can rest and recover," he said as he began moving an IV bag over to a pole on the bed and disconnecting the machine that was monitoring her pulse and blood pressure.

"You ready for a little ride?"

"I guess so," Gladys replied; "Cause I don't think I'm in any shape for a walk at the moment."

"Yeah, probably not today," he replied.

The nurse looked at Sam and said, "Are you going with us, Sir?"

"You bet," Sam quickly replied; "Primary care giver."

"Alrighty then," the nurse said, "let's get this show on the road."

He kicked a pedal under the bed to disengage the brakes and began rolling the bed towards the doorway. Sam followed the nurse as he pushed Gladys and her bed down the hallway towards a set of double doors. The nurse pushed a large metal button on the wall, and both doors opened for them. They proceeded down the hallway to an elevator lobby. He pushed the button and the three waited quietly. After a few silent minutes the elevator dinged and the arrow pointing up on the doorframe beside the elevator door lit up.

"Elevator up," said the nurse; "Ladies wear, shoes, handbags, and accessories."

He maneuvered Gladys' bed into the elevator and Sam followed them. The nurse pushed a button and the doors closed. The elevator made a little rumble under their feet and began rising. After a few more minutes, the elevator dinged again and the doors opened. The nurse rolled Gladys' bed out of the elevator and down the hallway stopping at a Nurse's Station.

"Morning, Morning," he said. "I have a special delivery for you."

An older lady rose from a seat behind the counter and said, "Who ya got for me there?"

The nurse looked at the clipboard hanging on the bedrail.

"Miss Gladys Boatwright," he reported. "She just had a hip fracture repaired and is looking forward to a relaxing vacation at the Orthopedic Villas and

Spa. She has requested comfortable accommodations overlooking the pool."

The older lady nurse grinned, "I think we have the garden room ready for her - 7023."

"Ya hear that Miss Gladys? They are giving you the garden room."

He rolled Gladys' bed to room 7023 and maneuvered it beside the bed in the room. He lowered the rails on the bed in the room and on the bed Gladys had been transported. The older lady nurse from the Nurse's Station walked in the door as he readied things to move Gladys from one bed to the other.

"Miss Gladys," the woman said, "Let us do the work. You probably aren't gonna like us for a few minutes for this, but once we get you moved onto the other bed, I have a pain med prescription for you that should win you back over."

Once they had the beds perfectly aligned, the male nurse locked the brakes on the bed where Gladys lay. Both nurses walked to the far side of the empty bed and positioned themselves.

"OK, Gladys," the older woman said, "You get a double handful of those covers and clench your teeth. We are going to pull the mat your lying on and slide you to your new bed."

Gladys grabbed two fists of the blanket that covered her.

The older woman looked at the male nurse and said, "Alright 1, 2, 3."

They pulled in unison and carefully slid Gladys from one bed to the other. Gladys let out a groan and then relaxed both hands.

"Alrighty dear," the older woman said; "Let's get you comfortable."

She gradually raised the head of Gladys' bed a few inches and then slightly lowered the foot of her bed so that her knees were ever-so-slightly bent.

"Is that better than flat on your back, dear?"

Gladys responded, "Yeah."

"OK, dear," she said; "Here is the remote. It has controls to raise and lower your head and feet to whatever is better for you. It also has the big red Nurse Call button on it. It also controls your television, the room lights, the window shades, and the heat. So you can set the room any way that makes you comfortable."

The male nurse unlocked the brakes on the transport bed and maneuvered it carefully towards the door.

"Miss Gladys," he said; "I hope you have a pleasant recovery. Get feeling better."

He rolled the bed out the doorway and out of sight.

The older woman walked to a whiteboard on the wall under the television across the room from Gladys' bed. She began writing on the board as she talked.

"My name is Christy. I am the head nurse on duty today. My nursing assistant is Katherine. We are glad you are on our wing, and we are going to do everything we can to make you comfortable and get you up and getting around as soon as possible. Don't you worry about a thing. We have been through this adventure with a couple hundred or so folks in the last couple of years, so we will get you through this smoothly."

Christy walked over to the IV pole and made an adjustment on the IV controller. She put a pulse oximeter on Gladys's finger and then put a blood pressure cuff around her upper arm. She pushed a few buttons on the controller on the IV pole and the blood pressure cuff began to inflate. When the controller beeped twice, she noted the readings on the controller and pushed a button to record the readings. She pulled a small electronic tablet up and made a few swipes on it.

"As promised, I am going to get you that pain med."

Christy walked out the door of the room. Sam walked over to the edge of the bed.

"Gladys," he said; "I'm still here. If you need or want anything, you just tell me and we will make it happen."

"Oh," Gladys said, "I thought you would have eased out when they rolled me up here. Thank you for staying, Pastor."

Sam smiled, "Like I said earlier, we are your family through this Gladys. We are here for you."

Sam walked over and sat down in a recliner that sat next to the head of the bed.

After a few minutes, Christy walked back in the door with a small bag in her hand.

"OK, Gladys," she said; "I have a cocktail for you to help you rest a little. In a couple of hours a Rehab Nurse is going to come visit and help you get ready to get back to walking."

Christy spiked the smaller bag and ran a line from it to the main IV line and then hung the smaller bag on the IV pole. She poked a couple of buttons on the IV controller and then looked back at Gladys.

"Let that pain medicine get in your system and you try to rest a bit. Maybe even sleep a little if you like. We will be in and out if you need us."

She walked over to Sam who rose to his feet.

"Hi and what is your name?" she asked.

He smiled and replied, "I'm Reverend Samuel Matthews. Gladys doesn't have any local family, so I am here for her."

"Very nice," Christy said, "I see your Grady Clergy badge, so you have been here a time or two. If we can do anything to make you comfortable, let us know. We have coffee, juices, sodas, and snacks for you at the Nurses Station if you want anything."

"Thank you," Sam replied, "That's very kind."

He sat back down in the recliner. Christy walked to the doorway.

"Alright Gladys," she said, "You rest a bit, and one of us will be back by to check on you."

Within a few minutes, the pain medications began to work and Gladys fell asleep.

Chapter 8

Ron Barlow had walked Jeff, his district manager, to his hotel on 17th Street after the two had eaten breakfast with the others who had sheltered the night at Peachtree Street Church. He was anxious to get back to 10th Street to check on his Charger. When they had abandoned it the night before, it still had gas, but it simply would not move due to the frozen street. He could see his breath in the cold air as he walked down the partially cleared sidewalk on the side of Peachtree Street. Seven blocks did not seem like much of a walk for him normally, but today's hike required his full attention to avoid ice patches and tree branches that had snapped under the weight of ice. Ron had always thought the Bradford Pear trees along Peachtree Street were beautiful, but today they were the worst of the casualties having lost the majority of their limbs filling parts of the sidewalk forcing him to walk in the street at times.

When Ron finally reached 10th Street, there were many of the abandoned cars that that had forced him to seek shelter. But some of the cars were gone. The wrecked MARTA bus and delivery truck that had caused the street blockage had been removed, and city workers had repaired the damaged fire hydrant water supply, or at least had it shut down. The weight of the vehicles used to tow the MARTA bus and delivery truck had done a lot to clear some significant ruts in the snow and ice for lighter cars like his to take advantage. As he got closer, he could see several people pushing a car toward the ruts while the driver spun tires anxiously seeking traction. When the car dropped into the ruts and started moving on its own, everyone let out a cheer.

When he reached the waiting Charger, it took a couple of firm tugs to separate car's door from the frozen seals. He crawled in and cranked the car and turned on the defrosters. He opened the trunk and retrieved an ice scraper and looked at Jeff's luggage still in his trunk.

"Bet he would like to have that at some point," Ron said to himself.

As the car's engine began to warm, Ron set about scraping the windshield, side windows, and rear windows as well as brushing snow off the cowl area and hood. As he worked, he could hear the group pushing another car from its snowy would-be-grave over to the ever-developing ruts, and then the predicable cheers of success when one more was free and on its way. Ron wondered how long they had been freeing cars along the street and if anyone was having comparable success on the interstates.

After getting all of the ice scraped off, the car windows were still pretty fogged up, so Ron had no choice but to wait for the car's defroster to clear the windshield. A small clear oval was beginning to form at the center of the base of the windshield, so at least progress was occurring, albeit slow. Ron looked up and took stock of the situation on the street. There were four cars directly in front of the Charger. The group was presently working on the first of the four, trying to get it moving towards the ruts. Since he had to wait before his car would be ready to even attempt to be moved, he figured he might as well lend a hand.

He walked up to the group as they were pushing on an 80's model Mustang. Without a word, Ron stepped in next to one of the group, braced against the car's trunk deck with both hands, steadied his feet as best as he could for traction and began pushing. The driver spun the tires desperately trying to gain traction as the group continued to struggle for footing and pushed. Finally the old car began to move, slowly. As the driver struggled to steer the car towards the ruts, the group assembled around it continued to struggle for footing while doing their best to push it. After several more minutes, the car finally fell into the tracks that had been worn into the frozen surface, and the old Mustang began to pull off. One of the group that had been pushing began running along the passenger side, managed to open the car door and jump inside. As the Mustang slowly pulled out of sight, what had previously been a loud cheer was now expressed as a group sigh of exhaustion. Ron looked at the remaining group - two men in their early 20s and a lady he guessed to be late 20s maybe early 30s. He looked at the next car in line in front of his.

"Does this Lexus belong to any of you?" Ron asked.

The woman quickly responded, "That would be mine. I thought we would never get to it," she said sounding exhausted.

She reached in the car and cranked it. The windows had already been scraped, so it seemed ready to be the next one freed from the icy grips of 10th Street.

"OK," Ron said, "turn the wheels toward the ruts, but don't turn them completely that way until we get you rolling. If you turn too quickly, we won't be able to get it moving."

"Gotcha," the woman said.

He looked at the other two men who looked physically spent.

"How long you guys been at this?"

A tall guy wearing a Georgia tech hooded sweatshirt responded, " A couple of hours or so, I guess. We've been trying to work our way back to our car," he said pointing at a Honda Prius between them and Ron's Charger.

Ron nodded in response.

"Ready to get this one out of your way?"

They both chuckled.

"Yeah man," the second one said.

The three men assumed positions behind the car and stomped their feet into the snow covered street to try and find traction so they could push the Lexus. As they began to push, one of them banged on the quarter panel.

"OK," he shouted, "Try it!"

The woman began spinning the wheels, but the car was not moving. The men pushed harder as she continued to spin the tires which only threw a spray of ice and slush covering their pants legs. Their feet were constantly slipping as they tried to push the Lexus, and they struggled to stay upright at the same time. The car just did not seem to want to move.

"Stop!" Ron shouted.

The woman stopped spinning the car's tires and the three men relaxed for a second. Ron walked to the front of the car to look at how the front tires were pointed. He knocked on the passenger window and the woman rolled it down.

"Straighten your wheels up and let's see if that helps," he suggested.

He walked to the rear of the car and assumed a position pushing on the trunk lid.

"Alright," hollered the guy in the Georgia Tech sweatshirt, "hit it!"

The tires on the Lexus began spinning again, and the three men began pushing once more. Ron was certain he could feel the car slowly beginning to move. They pushed it a couple of feet and the woman began slowly steering towards the ruts. After a few more minutes, the Lexus slowly approached the rutted area of the street and the front tires fell into the ruts. The three men shifted to the driver's side quarter panel and gave the car one more good shove and the rear tires fell into the tracks in the snow. The woman stepped on the accelerator again, and this time the Lexus began moving under its own power. She rolled the driver's side window down enough to stick a hand out and wave as she shouted a thank you. The Lexus slowly crawled out of sight. A cheer did not go up from the three tired men who stood motionlessly in the snow. In almost unison, the three turned and looked at the Prius sitting motionless and dark.

The guy in the Georgia Tech Sweatshirt trudged his way to the driver's door and tugged it a few times to gain entry. He started the car, flipped on the defroster, and began rummaging around the interior looking for an ice scraper. After a few minutes of frantic motion inside the car, he popped his head out of the driver's side doorway and called to Ron.

"Any chance I could use your ice scraper?" he asked sheepishly.

"I got ya," Ron replied and walked back to the Charger which now set idling with perfectly clear windows. Ron retrieved his ice scraper and walked to the Prius.

"You guys look spent," he said. "Y'all crawl in and thaw out for a minute. I'll get the windows for you."

The two men crawled into the car without putting up a fuss. Ron set about scraping windows. When he reached the rear of the car, he heard a noise and turned to locate the source. He could see a small headlight coming towards them from Peachtree Street. Four-wheeler ATV, Ron figured. He began scraping the back window and continued to watch the approaching headlight. As he finished scraping ice, a four-wheeled ATV pulled up in front of them. A tall figure wearing a heavy green parka stepped off the ATV and approached him.

"Hello Sir," said a male voice from under a fur lined hood; "National Guard. Would you like some help getting this car moving?"

"You bet we would," Ron replied.

The man pulled up the seat on the ATV and retrieved a tow strap. As he walked to the front of the car, the two men stepped out of the car. They began to dig in the snow in front of the Prius to try and locate a place to connect the tow strap.

"I'm going to let y'all hook that up since it's your car, said the National Guardsman. "I am not assuming any responsibility for any damage yanking on it."

"No problem," shouted one of the two men from under the front of the car.

After a few minutes, they both stood up and began brushing snow off of their clothes.

The young man in the Georgia Tech sweatshirt breathlessly spoke up, "I think we got it. Let's give it a try."

He crawled back into the driver seat while Ron and the other young man took positions at the back of the car. Again they stomped their feet into the snow seeking to find firm footing. The ATV pulled the tow strap tight and the Prius began to spin its tiny front tires. The two men began pushing as the ATV began revving its engine. Slowly the snow and ice released its grip on the Prius to the forces of the tugging ATV and the pushing of two tired men. The ATV began to gain the advantage and the two men stopped pushing as it pulled the Prius into the ruts plowed into the slush by all of the previous traffic. The young man that had been pushing with Ron scrambled to the front of the Prius and lay down in the street to disconnect the tow strap. Once he had it disconnected from the car, he carried it to the ATV and coiled it on the rear luggage rack.

"Thanks for y'alls help," the young man said as he crawled into the passenger side of the car.

He closed his door, and Ron watched the Prius pull out of sight. He turned and looked at the Charger and then back at the National Guardsman on the ATV.

"Guess it's just us now," Ron said.

He began walking back to the Charger as the ATV made a U-turn in the street and began driving towards him. Ron was not terribly enthused by the prospect of crawling under the front of the car in the snow to try and find a point of attachment for the tow strap, but he certainly preferred to sleep in his own bed tonight as opposed to another night on a military cot. He began digging into the snow. The ATV pulled up in front of the car and began idling. Ron dug a hole in the snow enough to expose the center of the car. He took the end of the tow strap and hooked it to a point on the lower front suspension.

"Alright," he said, standing up and beating the snow and slush off his clothes; "Let's see what we've got."

He crawled in the car, put it in gear and gently stepped on the accelerator. The back tires began to spin and the rear of the car began to dance side to side a bit trying to find traction. He could hear the engine on the ATV begin to rev as it pulled. He continued to spin the rear tires of the Charger and moved the steering wheel back and forth, trying to help the car find any minute amount of traction. Finally it began to move. The rear tires continued to spin, but the car was slowly moving forward. After a few more minutes of slow progress, Ron could feel the front wheels fall into the ruts in the street. The ATV continued to pull. Ron stepped on the accelerator a little harder spinning the wheels and then steered the car enough to make the rear-end spin sideway and over into the ruts. He honked the horn to let the soldier on the ATV know he could stop. Ron crawled out of the car, knelt in the snow, and disconnected the tow strap. He pulled the glove off his right hand and extended it to the soldier on the ATV. The soldier quickly removed his glove and shook his hand.

"I greatly appreciate the help," Ron said. "I'd have been out here on my own without your help."

"Glad I could help, Sir," the soldier replied. "Be safe out there."

The young soldier disconnected the tow strap from the back of the ATV, stowed it beneath the seat, and remounted the machine. He dropped it in gear and headed further down 10th Street. Ron returned to the warm Charger, closed the door, removed his gloves, and slowly headed to Peachtree Street.

"I'll drop Jeff's bags off at his hotel and then I'm going home," he said to himself.

Chapter 9

Jeff brushed snow off his pants legs and stomped his feet to get as much of the slush off his shoes before walking into the hotel lobby. He walked through the automatic double sliding doors that opened as he approached them. He walked across the tile-floored lobby to the check-in counter. A young man sporting a shirt and tie greeted him as he approached.

"Checking in?"

"Yes, Sir," Jeff responded. "I was supposed to check in yesterday afternoon, but got stuck in traffic and spent the night in an Emergency Shelter. Is my room still available?"

"Let me check for you, Sir," the young man replied; "What name is the reservation under?"

"Jeff Treadwell," Jeff replied.

The young man punched away at the keyboard on the computer behind the counter.

"Yes, Sir," the young man replied after a few minutes. "Your room was guaranteed for late arrival, and we held it for you. Would you like to charge the room against the credit card that it was reserved against?"

"Yes, please," Jeff replied almost automatically.

The young man pulled out a pair of door swipe cards, inserted them into a piece of equipment on the counter top and punched a code on a keypad on the front of the machine. Jeff heard a distinct "thunk" sound and the machine then ejected both cards.

"Here you go, Sir," the young man said.

He slid the key cards in a small bi-fold pamphlet. He wrote the room number on the back of the pamphlet.

"Your room number is 786. Elevator is down the hall and on the right. You are on the seventh floor. We serve a complimentary breakfast from 6am until 10am across the way in the lobby. Complimentary coffee, cappuccinos, and juices are available 24 hours. If you have forgotten any toiletry items, we have complimentary spares available here at the front desk."

Jeff took the bi-fold pamphlet and proceeded down the hall to the elevator. He pushed the call button on the wall next to the elevator door and patiently waited. After a few minutes, he heard the ding of the elevator and the up indicator next to the elevator door lit up. The doors opened and he stepped into the elevator. He pushed the number seven and a circle lit up around the button. The doors closed and he felt a slight rumble under his feet as the elevator began to ascend. After a few more minutes, the elevator dinged again and an LCD panel next to the door displayed the number seven. The doors opened and Jeff looked around. He located a sign indicating room number ranges, and headed to the right towards his room. After a brief stroll down the hallway, he was at his room door. He slid the door swipe card into the door lock and the pulled it out. He heard a click and a green light on the door lock illuminated. He pushed down on the handle and opened the door. He walked into the room, flipped on a light switch. He walked over to a comfortable looking upholstered wingback chair and flopped his tired frame into it. He reached into his coat pocket and retrieved his cell phone. He pushed a button.

"Siri," he said; "Dial Jan."

The phone dialed the number and his wife answered on the third ring.

"Jeff?"

"Hey honey," Jeff replied; "I finally got to my hotel. Ron is going to be bringing my bags shortly."

"Thank heavens! We've been watching the news and it looks like the whole town is shutdown."

"Yeah," he continued, "I bet there were over 500 people in that shelter last night. Atlanta apparently has a pretty large homeless population. So in addition to all of the stranded travelers there last night, I talked to several homeless. From what they told me, there are more homeless on any given night than there are beds in homeless shelters. So, the individuals I met last night forego trying to get into a shelter on normal nights, but the weather forced them to seek shelter last night."

"That's terrible," Jan replied; "I can't imagine having nowhere to sleep at night and being subjected to the elements."

"Exactly," Jeff continued; "Something needs to be done. It got me thinking. Corporate does a lot of sponsorships and a lot of community involvement projects. I think they need to look into how we as a company could get involved in a solution to homelessness in Atlanta."

"That would be a terrific idea," his wife replied.

"Well," he said, "I wanted to check in and let you and the kids know I am alright. Ron should be by with my bags in a bit. Then I am going to get a hot shower and see if I can find some dinner."

"Alright," she said, "I love you, honey. Stay safe."

"I love you too, Sweetie," he replied, "Good night."

He hung up the phone and slid it in his coat pocket and closed his eyes for a minute.

Chapter 10

Ron slowly drove North on Peachtree Street ever thankful for the heat coming out under the dash of the Charger. When he reached 17th Street, he pulled into the circular driveway in front of the hotel. He put the car in park and dialed Jeff's number on his cellphone.

Jeff answered on the second ring, "Hey buddy."

Ron replied, "I'm downstairs in the driveway with your bags."

"Awesome," Jeff replied; "I'll be down in a second."

Ron hung up his phone and tucked it back in his coat pocket. In a few minutes, he saw Jeff appear through the automatic sliding doors of the hotel lobby. He punched the trunk release button, and crawled out of the car. He walked around to the trunk and retrieved Jeff's bags setting them on the brick pavers just behind the Charger.

"Thanks for this," Jeff said as he extended the handles on both bags.

"No problem," Ron replied, "Get some rest and have a good night."

"You too," Jeff responded.

Ron watched him as he walked back to the lobby with the bags rolling along behind him. Once Jeff was inside the lobby, Ron walked back to the driver's side of the Charger, opened the door and crawled back under the steering wheel. He closed the door, pulled his seatbelt across his chest and latched it, and slid the shifter into drive.

"Let's go home," he said to himself; "Finally."

He pulled the Charger out of the hotel drive, maneuvered back to Peachtree Street and headed North to continue a trip that he had started the prior afternoon. He flipped on the radio to WSB and began listening to the news of continued power outages, downed trees, fallen limbs in roadways, and the mess that was the interstates. Captain Herb Emory gave a report from the WSB traffic helicopter as he flew over Atlanta's interstates. Slowly but surely wrecks were being cleared, and plows were beginning to clear lanes.

The drive was oddly eerie to Ron. He had made this trip a few thousand times and had always enjoyed the city lights as he drove through town. But tonight was different. The buildings were all dark, very few lights were shining, and many of the traffic signals were out. It was almost like a completely different city that he had never seen. Every intersection was an adventure. Many of those out and about were not familiar with how to handle an intersection without operational traffic lights. Ron remembered that in those cases, you treated the intersection as a four way stop. The first car that stopped had the right of way. If two cars stopped at the same time, the one to the right had the right of way. It seemed pretty simple to Ron, but it was perplexing to many of the other drivers who stopped, looked at each other and then began waving.

"Where did these people learn to drive?" he said out loud.

After almost an hour, Ron completed the short drive from 17th Street to his townhouse.

"I bet I know a little dog that is about to burst," he thought.

He pulled the Charger into the townhouse's single car garage and closed the garage door. He opened the stairway door and began climbing the stairs to the main level.

"Buzz! Where are you buddy?"

He heard a jingle of tags on a dog collar and then the familiar thump of paws galloping on a hardwood floor. A Bassett hound appeared out of the darkness with his tail wagging violently.

"I bet you need to go out, don't you buddy?" Ron said to the dog.

He reached for a leash hanging on the wall just outside the kitchen and knelt down. He rubbed Buzz's head and the tail wagging increased in speed. He clipped the leash onto Buzz's collar and led him down the stairs to the front door. Once outside, Buzz's paws stopped at the edge of the porch, and he inquisitively sniffed at the snow lying on the ground in front of him. He then cautiously stepped into the snow, one paw then the other until he was standing on the snow covered lawn. Buzz began sniffing around before finding the perfect spot, the lamppost at the edge of the curbing. He hiked his hind leg and began to empty the contents of his bladder. Ron thought it would never end.

"You been holding that for a while ain't ya buddy?"

Buzz looked back at him over his shoulder still holding his hind leg in the air. Finally completing the task, Buzz dropped his leg and snorted almost in disgust. He turned and bounded for the door. Once on the porch, he shook himself from head to tail as hard as he could to rid himself of the cold snow and slush. He stopped with his nose on the door to the townhouse and looked at Ron over his shoulder. Ron quickly opened the door, unclipped the leash, and Buzz ran up the stairs. When Ron reached the top of the stairs, Buzz was sitting in front of the cabinet under the kitchen sink with one front paw held up in a begging position. Ron chuckled.

"Yeah, that was a good boy," he said.

Ron opened the cabinet door, reached into a box, retrieved a dog treat, and gave it to Buzz. Buzz's tail wagged with delight as he munched away on his treat. Ron patted him on the head. He unlaced his snow and slosh stained shoes and set them by the door to the garage. He hung his coat in the hallway closet and then headed up the stairs to the master bedroom. He walked into the bathroom, reached into the shower and turned on the hot water. He peeled off his cold damp socks and then stripped off the rest of his clothes and tossed them into a hamper by the bedroom door. He stepped into the shower and stood motionless as the hot water ran across his cold and tired muscles. He wondered how long he could stand there before the hot water gave out. He shrugged off the thought, shampooed his hair, lathered his body, and rinsed; pausing to let the hot water run across his tired muscles one more time before shutting the water off. He grabbed a huge fluffy towel and dried himself off.

"Man it feels good to get a hot shower again," he thought to himself. He had only been a day without the convenience. He thought about some of the homeless people he and Jeff had met at the emergency shelter. One of the guys told him that sometimes it was a month before he had the opportunity to take a shower. He pulled on a pair of fleece pajama bottoms and a long-sleeved Atlanta Falcons t-shirt and flipped out all of the lights. He crawled into his bed thankful to be home, safe, and warm. He heard a jingle as Buzz climbed the carpeted ramp at the end of the bed and crawled up and lay down at his feet. Within a matter of minutes, Ron was asleep with Buzz slightly snoring at the food of the bed.

Chapter 11

Joy put the car in park and shut off the old Honda's engine. She opened the car door, carefully stepped out, and searched for secure footing. Steadying herself against the car, she locked the door and then carefully began walking toward the gym's main entrance. Fortunately, someone had cleared the sidewalk and salted it to prevent it from refreezing. When she opened the lobby door to the gym, she was instantly greeted with the roar of several hundred children. She secretly pitied the teachers and coaches who listened to that level of ambient noise daily for a living. As she approached the doors leading into the gym from the lobby, she was greeted by two ladies seated at a folding table.

"Good Afternoon," said the first lady; "Name?"

"Hi," Joy replied. "Joy Davidson. Here to pick up Cheryl and Jeremy Davidson."

The woman looked down a clipboard for a moment, moving her lips silently as she read names.

"Ah," she remarked. "Here you are. Can I see a driver's license or another form of photo ID, please?"

Joy was already prepared for the request, and had retrieved her driver's license from her purse.

"Here you go," Joy said.

The woman looked at the license, ran her finger across it and then looked back at the clipboard.

OK, sign right here, please," she said, handing the clipboard to Joy.

Joy signed next to both children's names and handed the clipboard back to the woman who handed Joy her driver's license back. Joy stowed her driver's license back in her purse and pulled the strap back up on her shoulder.

"This way please," the woman said.

She led Joy into the Gym and over to where one of the coaches was sitting on the edge of the bleachers.

"Coach Johnson, Ms. Davidson to pickup Cheryl and Jeremy Davidson, please."

The man stood to his feet.

"Alrighty," he said.

The woman turned and headed back to the lobby. The coach picked up a cordless Public Address Microphone, turned it upside down and flipped a switch. He turned it right side up and then spoke into the microphone in a booming voice.

"Cheryl and Jeremy Davidson, your mother is here to pick you up," he announced.

He turned the microphone back upside down and flipped the switch off. Joy wondered why he needed a microphone with that booming voice, but said nothing. Out of the corner of her eye, she saw some bustling. She turned towards the commotion to see Cheryl scrambling to put her jacket on and Jeremy walking towards his little sister carrying his jacket and book bag. Joy began walking towards Cheryl.

"MAMA!" Cheryl exclaimed, running to greet her with a hug while dragging her jacket with one arm in one sleeve and the other out.

Joy reached down and hugged her and helped her finish putting on her jacket. Jeremy walked up.

"Hey Mom, how is it outside?"

Joy shook her head.

"It was an adventure getting up the hill in our Honda," she said with a smile.

"Yeah," Jeremy replied, "Coach said earlier you couldn't get up it without a four wheel drive."

Joy laughed, "Somebody forgot to tell me that! Put on your jacket and let's get ready to roll."

"Sounds good," Jeremy replied; "My bed is a lot more comfortable than this gym."

The children collected their belongings and followed Joy out to the lobby.

"Thank you ladies," Joy said as she passed the ladies seated at the folding table who were checking in another pair of parents.

"Y'all be safe," one of the ladies called out.

The three walked to the Honda dutifully waiting at the curb like a tired old friend. Joy unlocked the car and the children crawled in the back seat. Joy crawled in under the steering wheel and started the car and the heater.

"So Mom," Jeremy started like so many times before, "I learned something interesting last night."

"Oh really," Joy said; "And what was that?"

"Well I said something how I wish I was sleeping in my bed at home last night, and a couple of the kids told me they don't have beds at home."

"What?" Joy replied.

She could not imagine it. She had struggled providing for the children as a single parent at times, sometimes doing without things herself to ensure their needs were provided. She could not imagine them not having a bed in which to sleep.

"Yeah," he continued; "One kids parents separated, and he's been sleeping on the floor in his bedroom of their apartment ever since. The other kid said his Dad lost a job and they had to move in with his Granny. So, his Dad has a bed, his sister has the sofa, and he is sleeping on the floor."

Cheryl perked up at the conversation.

"My friend Carlese doesn't have a bed," she volunteered.

Joy looked in the mirror. "Carlese that lives downstairs from our apartment?"

"Yes Ma'am," Cheryl replied. "She was having a hard time staying awake in class one day. So I asked her what was wrong. She said she doesn't sleep well at night, because she is sleeping on the floor. She has a sister and two brothers, and they don't have beds either. So I asked her why she didn't sleep on the sofa. She said they don't have one. She said they don't have any furniture. So I asked her where do you sit to eat? She said they sit on the floor of the living room."

Joy shook her head and looked back up in the mirror.

"When you say your prayers tonight, I think you both should say a 'Thank You' for your warm beds," Joy suggested.

Jeremy smiled, "Already on my list. Those gym mats weren't much to brag about."

Joy quietly wondered if the people at Peachtree Street Church might be able to help with some children's beds. The preacher had given her his card and said to call if they ever needed anything.

"How about if the neighbor kids needed anything," she thought.

She decided to give him a call when things got back to normal, and see what he could recommend. After safely navigating back down the hill, she drove the short route back to their apartment complex and up to their building.

"Boy am I glad to see this place," Cheryl said looking up.

"Yeah," said Jeremy, "me too."

"You aren't the only ones," Joy added, "I slept on an Army cot in a Sunday School classroom last night."

"Neat!" said Cheryl.

Joy laughed.

"It wasn't quite the adventure you might imagine, Cheryl," she commented; "But it was better than sleeping in the car!"

Joy led the kids inside their apartment and sighed in relief to finally be home. She felt blessed to find the power was on and the apartment was warm.

"Ok, you both need to take a shower and change into some clean clothes." she told them.

"First dibs on the bathroom," Cheryl shouted and took off running.

Joy sat down on the sofa and thought to herself how good it felt. She closed her eyes for a moment and thought about what Cheryl had told her about her friend Carlese and her family living in an apartment without furniture. She could completely understand how it could happen. The struggle to pay rent and utilities, buy groceries, and keep her two children clothed was a never-ending one. Single parents were faced with difficult decisions every day. Choices had to be made and priorities had to be set. A safe, warm, dry place to sleep took priority over luxuries and creature comforts. Keeping the lights and heat on was higher on the list than a dining room table or a 50-inch flat screen.

As she thought about it, her mind went back to school. Maslow's hierarchy of needs - that was it! The first level of needs was physiological. First, a person needed air, water, food, clothing, and shelter from the elements. That was what Carlese's family was addressing as best as they could with the financial resources they had available. Furnishings for the apartment added comfort, but when push came to shove, addressing those primary needs came first. But there was a cost. Someone sleeping on the floor would mean a person wouldn't get a good night's rest and would wake up groggy and exhausted. Poor quality of sleep would negatively affect a child's performance in school and an adult's performance at work. It could lead to a child falling asleep in class or struggling to pay attention.

Joy wished that she had the means to go out and buy beds for Carlese's family, but she was barely covering her own with two growing children. She was jarred from the thought by Cheryl bouncing into her lap.

"Dry my hair for me, Please!" she begged of Joy.

Joy grabbed the towel draped across her small shoulders and began to dry her hair. By the time Joy had Cheryl's hair dry, she could hear the dull thump of Jeremy's feet coming down the hallway.

"Ok, y'all," Joy said, "It's been a long couple of days. I want both of you to get a good night's sleep."

"I'm alright," Jeremy piped up.

"Well," Joy began to reconsider. "There is no school tomorrow. I guess you could stay up a little while. But you better be in bed by midnight, mister."

"Score!" Jeremy exclaimed.

He plopped down on the sofa beside her and picked up the remote.

"Cheryl" Joy continued, "You, Little Miss, need to get in the bed."

"Yes um," Cheryl quickly responded.

She crawled up in her mother's lap and gave her a huge hug.

"Let's get you tucked in," Joy said, picking her up and starting towards the bedroom.

"Mama," Cheryl said looking up at Joy as she carried her down the hallway. "I want to figure out some way to get Carlese a bed."

"Me too, Princess," Joy said. "I've been thinking about that ever since you told me about it. I don't have anything figured out yet, but I'm thinking about it."

Joy laid Cheryl on her bed and flipped off the ceiling light. She could make out her daughter's face from the dim light of the nightlight across the room. Cheryl's eyes were closed. Joy sat down on the edge of the bed, and Cheryl began to pray.

"Dear God," Cheryl said in a soft voice, "Thank you for getting us all home safe. Thank you for my warm bed and my mama and brother. Please bless Carlese with a bed so she can sleep at night and make better grades in school. Amen."

Joy leaned over and kissed her on the forehead.

"Good night, Princess," Joy said softly, "I love you."

"I love you too, Mama!"

Joy stood and slowly walked to the door. She quietly closed the door and returned to the living room where Jeremy sat fixated on the television.

"I'm going to bed," she called to Jeremy who quickly glanced up at her.

"Don't forget," she reminded him; "In bed by midnight. If I wake up after midnight, and I hear that television, there will be problems."

"Yes ma'am," he replied without looking up from his television-induced trance.

"Goodnight, Son," she said. "I love you."

Jeremy did not respond. Joy turned back down the hallway to her room and retired for the night.

Chapter 12

Just after 11pm, Samuel Mathews was sitting in the lounge area just across from the nurses' station sipping a cup of coffee and reading his Bible when a man approached him. Sam looked up at the approaching figure and tried to focus his eyes. He removed his wire-rimmed glasses and rubbed his tired eyes. He put his glasses back on and attempted to focus on the man that was now less than 6 feet away. For a moment, Sam thought he was dreaming. The man now standing before him was the living image of Santa Claus dressed in a faded shirt and camouflage pants carrying a large sack on his shoulders. It was well after Christmas, and Sam felt foolish even entertaining the idea of Santa Claus. But the grey haired gent with the long grey full beard and a large sack on his shoulders looked like he had stepped out of a Hallmark card - minus the traditional red suit of course.

"Reverend Mathews?" the man asked lifting one eyebrow.

Sam scrambled to his feet.

"Yes, Sir," Sam replied.

The man set his large sack on the floor.

"Sir," the man said; "My name is Lewis Davis. This is going to sound like a bit of a strange story, but please bear with me. I am a homeless Vet. I have lived on the streets of this city for more years than I want to acknowledge. Anyway, Miss Gladys is a friend of mine. We frequent the same building and cross each other's path practically daily. I was one of the people who found her in the snow the other night. I talked with my friend Fred, another homeless man that I see a lot on the streets. We both sheltered at your church during the storm. He told me he thought you were sitting with Gladys. I had a bit of a time finding where she was in this hospital, but finally found y'all. I wanted to check on Miss Gladys and see if you or she needed anything."

Sam sat dumbfounded for a moment. A homeless man was checking to see if he needed anything? It seemed like some weird role reversal to him. He was a pastor. He should be coming to the aid of the homeless man. This man had walked several miles in frigid weather to check on Gladys and him. Sam was caught off-guard by the generosity of someone who had practically nothing but the clothes on his back. Finally he spoke.

"That is very kind of you," Sam said. "You must be frozen to the core after walking all the way here from the church. How about a cup of coffee? They keep a fresh pot brewing right around the corner here."

"Alright," Lewis said, "That would be good."

Lewis nodded. Sam led him to the coffee maker and poured Lewis a cup.

Lewis looked up from his coffee and said, "Is there anything I can do for you? Do you have anyone to switch off with while you're sitting with her?"

Sam shook his head.

"No. Honestly I didn't make any real plan. I just knew the National Guard was sitting with her while she went through surgery and eventually she'd be sitting up here alone," Sam explained. "I just couldn't stand the thought of that."

Lewis nodded his affirmation.

"Well, Sir," Lewis responded, "With her breaking a hip, she is gonna be here and then in physical therapy for a while. You aren't gonna be able to do this alone. I figure we need a woman that can change shifts sitting with her. I think I know someone who would be willing to help."

Sam listened intently.

"I have her number in my cell," Lewis continued. "Her name is Karen. She is a homeless advocate that volunteers at the Atlanta Mission."

Lewis pulled a flip phone out of a coat pocket, opened it and began to scroll through the directory.

"Here she is," he said pushing the dial button. Karen answered on the third ring.

"Miss Karen," he said, "This is Santa."

Sam smiled and shook his head.

"Do you remember Gladys, the lady who always has her hair up in a scarf and sits outside Chick-Fil-A at Colony Square most days?"

"Oh, yes," Karen answered, "I know her. I helped her get some shoes a couple weeks back."

"Well," Lewis continued; "She fell during the storm and suffered a broken hip. She's down here at Grady recovering from surgery. Pastor Mathews from Peachtree Street Church and I are up here sitting with her. I was wondering if you could help out rotating shifts with us sitting with her."

"Of course I will," Karen quickly replied. "Give the preacher my number. In fact, let me get a few things together and I will head down that way."

"Thank you," Lewis responded. "How about you get a night's rest and plan on coming in the morning? We can cover the watch tonight. I just got here myself."

"Ok," Karen said, "But don't hesitate to call me if you need me before then."

"Will do," Lewis said. "Good night."

"Good night, Santa", Karen said.

Lewis hung up the phone and looked at Reverend Mathews.

"She wants you to have her phone number," Lewis said.

"Oh, alright," Sam replied, and began digging into his inside jacket pocket. He retrieved an address book and a pen. Lewis read the number to him while Sam jotted it in the book.

"She is coming first thing in the morning to sit with Gladys so you can go home and get some rest," Lewis reported.

"That's wonderful," Sam replied. "I didn't have any real plan. In fact I rode here with the National Guard so I don't even have transportation home."

Lewis nodded and smiled, "We will worry with details in the morning."

Sam nodded in agreement.

"So, Lewis," Sam said, "tell me your story."

Lewis looked up at him after taking a long sip of his coffee.

"I was your run of the mill high school kid," Lewis started. "Nothing special. I played football but never got a scholarship to play college ball, so I joined the Army. They sent me overseas to some of the hottest and most humid jungles I ever imagined. I did three tours, made Sergeant, and a bullet to the leg sent me home. Once I got out of the VA hospital, I really couldn't get a good start at things. I worked construction jobs as a general laborer for 20 years, but fell off a roof one day and broke my back. Ran up a hell of a bill in the hospital with surgery, physical therapy and all. I didn't have any insurance and the hospital put the bill collectors on me. What little I had they got and the State of Georgia ruled I wasn't disabled. So, I couldn't work construction with the issues with my back. I started working little odd jobs which were hard to come by and made very little money. I began sleeping in shelters. I got the hell beat out of me in a couple and robbed. So I decided I wasn't sleeping in them anymore. So for the last six or seven years, I've been sleeping in doorways and under bridges and such - wherever the city cops will leave me alone. I guess you'd say this isn't the retirement I imagined for myself, but here I am. This ol' rucksack holds everything I own."

Sam listened intently without commenting.

Lewis continued, "Miss Gladys there, I seen her a lot when I get meals at the mission and when we get one of the gift cards folks donate. On colder days, we both sit in the food court of Colony Square during the day to stay warm.

Their security folks don't tend to harass us, we can both generally come up with a couple of bucks for something to eat there. Fred usually hangs out in the soft chairs in the Starbucks there. I have seen him around for years. We three kinda check on each other, but we don't sit in a bunch together as it draws too much attention. Attention when you're homeless results in you getting bounced out of a warm building. So, we sit tables apart and keep to ourselves to maintain a low profile."

Sam continued to listen. When he was confident Lewis was finished, he looked him straight in the eyes.

"Lewis," he said, "I really want to know the best way to make a difference in the lives of the homeless community in this city. I've always wondered what I could do. The Mission seems to do a good job, but it seems like the homeless community is so much larger than what they are equipped to address. If you were given the money to address the homeless situation in this city, what would you do different?"

Lewis thought for a while, stroking his beard as he contemplated the question. After several minutes of complete silence, he began to answer.

"Well," he said, "I never have liked shelters, because you never had your own space. You were always in a room with 3 or more other folks. And I don't mean to come off as ungrateful, but there's got to be some way to retain your dignity. Showering with 20 other guys … you know if somehow you could give each person their own space. Be it however small, their own space … where they could feel safe and get some rest without having to try to sleep light to protect your belongings and your own safety. And if I really wanted to just get crazy dreaming, I'd like to see nurses or doctors volunteer to address medical needs. Many of us are older, some are diabetic, some have asthma, you name it. Yeah, that would be pretty good if there was some way to do all that."

Sam listened and considered what Lewis was telling him.

"Instead of a huge building with bunks and large showers, maybe something like if someone renovated one of the old one or two story motels. Each person would have their own room and own bathroom. You'd have to figure something out for meals. But, they'd have a permanent address which is important for getting any kind of government assistance, and it would help to recruit medical volunteers. They would know where to find folks and could check on them regularly," Sam said.

Lewis nodded in agreement.

"Or maybe like if someone renovated a trailer park where each person had a trailer. They'd have a kitchen, bathroom, and everything," Lewis added.

Sam nodded as Lewis talked.

"In either scenario, the people establish a permanent address which also helps with finding work for those who aren't disabled," Lewis continued. "There are a lot of homeless folks who can work and want to work, but it is hard to meet dress codes and such for a lot of jobs if you are living on the street."

Sam looked up and said, "Lewis, I want to figure out how we do something like this. If I have to retire from the church, launch an organization, and start fundraising so be it. But, something needs to be done. I'm half expecting some backlash from the church for opening up a shelter in the light of the church's financial situation. But it was the right thing to do. And if they decided I put them in a financial hardship and decide to dismiss me, I'll walk out knowing I did the right thing. But this was just a drop of water on the tongue of a thirsty man. Opening the church as a shelter during the storm helped for a couple of days, but what about the other 363 days? We return to status quo and act like there aren't people needing shelter just outside our doors?"

Lewis was staring at Sam.

"You don't actually think they would fire you for opening up the church as a shelter do you?" Lewis asked in bewilderment.

"I honestly don't know," Sam quickly replied. "The finances have been so tight we haven't been able to do more than just a Sunday morning service.

The utility bill for heating the education wing and the sanctuary for the last two days will more than likely exceed what we normally spend in an entire month. The treasurer will probably have a stroke when the bill comes in. He'll call the head of the board who will then call me. Who knows what will happen from there. But you know, I'm not troubled by all that. I'm trying to find a path to serve the community right outside our doors. That community has changed significantly in the last 20 years, but our church hasn't. The community's needs have changed, but our church hasn't made any changes to address them.

Years ago, Martin Luther felt the Catholic Church had gone astray, and he nailed a list of grievances on the door of the church. It eventually spawned a reformation. Several days ago, a man froze to death on the steps of our church, and to me it is almost like the community nailed a list of grievances on our door. I believe we have to do something. Our lack of funding doesn't absolve us of our responsibility to care for the hurting outside our doors."

Both men sat in silence, contemplating their thoughts. Eventually, Lewis broke the silence.

"Where would we find a trailer park or an old motor lodge in Atlanta these days?" he asked. "I don't think I've seen a trailer park anywhere in the city. And the last motor lodge I remember was torn down years ago to build a high rise."

"Right," Sam replied. "If we were to do something like this, we would have to find property away from downtown. The suburbs all still have trailer parks and older two story motels. But the homeless community would have to be willing to relocate away from the inner city."

"Well", Lewis said, "I would wager that there's a good many of us that would be willing to make the move if we knew it meant we would regain our dignity and have security."

Chapter 13

John woke as the sun rose over the city. He looked at the fuel gauge on his truck and could see he still had an eighth of a tank left. The heater was still keeping the cab warm. He looked over in the passenger seat at the lady whose car behind him had run out of gas and her baby sleeping soundly. He looked out the windshield and could see in the distance crews working to move a tractor-trailer jackknifed in the roadway. As he sat watching them work, he began to hear a familiar sound - ATVs. He began to look around trying to locate them. They were getting closer. After a few minutes, he saw headlights in the rearview mirror. ATVs maneuvering through the abandoned cars. He stepped out of the cab of his truck, and one of the ATVs came to a halt behind his truck.

"Good Morning, Sir," said a female voice from under the hood of a heavy parka. "National Guard. Anyone out of gas or need a jump start?"

"Yeah," John quickly answered," He pointed to the lady's car behind him. "That car is out of gas and the lady and her baby are asleep in my truck."

"Alright," said the woman, "Let's see if we can get her started. The gas station at the top of the ramp is open, so if we can get her started and up that ramp, she should be good to go."

"Sweet!" John exclaimed.

He walked back up to the passenger door on his truck and tapped on the glass with a knuckle. He slowly opened the door.

"Ma'am," he said, "The National Guard is here and they have fuel to get your car started. Could I get your keys and see if we can get it cranked?"

The woman groggily responded, "I left the keys in the ignition. I didn't think there was much chance of anyone stealing it with it out of gas."

John chuckled. "Good point," he said.

He closed the door and walked back to the car. The woman from the ATV had a funnel in the car's gas tank filler neck and was hoisting a jerry jug pouring gas into the tank. After several minutes, she lowered the jug, removed the funnel, and fastened the gas cap.

"Alright, Sir," she said, "Let's see if she'll crank."

John crawled in the car and turned the key. He waited for several minutes for the fuel pump to pump fuel from the tank up to the engine. Then he turned the key to start. The engine began turning over. It coughed a couple of times. He tried again. The engine gave one more cough and then started. He lightly revved the engine to ensure it had ample fuel pressure and then crawled back out.

"I think she is good," John shouted back to the woman strapping the jug back onto the ATV.

"Good deal," said the woman; "On to the next!"

John walked back up to his truck. He looked up ahead to see a large loader had pulled the tractor-trailer off the edge of the interstate. Cars were slowly beginning to maneuver past. He knocked on the passenger door window again and then opened the door.

"Ma'am," he said, "We got your car started." He pointed to the off ramp just ahead on the right.

"There's an open gas station just up that ramp. And it looks like they have it salted where you can get up it," he said.

The woman began to climb out of the truck cab while holding the baby in her arms. John helped her back to her car and got them settled back into the car, which was quickly getting warm. A couple cars to their right began moving. John held up his arms and motioned one behind the line to stop, so the woman could pull over into the line. The car obliged and the woman pulled behind the slowly moving line. He stood in the cold watching her inch her way to the ramp and then slowly proceed up the ramp and out of sight. He walked back to the cab of his truck.

"Wonder if that station has any diesel," He said out loud to himself.

He figured it would be a good idea to fill the truck up as the ride could take more fuel than normal at the creepy crawly pace. He navigated his way over into the slow line and eventually up the ramp. When he reached the station, it was busy with cars fueling. He looked around but the woman and baby apparently had come and gone. He looked around and to his pleasant surprise, he saw a green handled nozzle on an end pump signifying diesel fuel. He pulled in line behind the pump and waited. After a few minutes he reached the pump and filled the truck. From the station, he could see the slow crawling line of cars on the interstate below. While the interstate was five lanes wide in each direction, he could only see two lanes that were moving.

"I'm not getting back into that mess," he thought.

After returning the nozzle to the pump and twisting the fuel cap on the truck's tank, John crawled back in the warm cab. He pointed the truck for Peachtree Street.

"Let's try some side streets and back roads," he said to himself.

He punched the button on the steering wheel.

"Call Mary," he said.

"Dialing Mary using OnStar," the system responded.

Mary answered on the first ring.

"Hey Sunshine," he said; "I'm finally off the interstate. I got a tank of fuel and am gonna start up Peachtree."

"That's probably your best bet," Mary replied, "They're still trying to clear a lot of tractor-trailer jams on all of the interstates."

"Yeah," John answered, "so give me a few hours, and I should be home."

"Love you, honey," she said.

"Love you, too, Doll," he replied and pushed the button on the steering wheel to disconnect the call.

He slowly began the drive North on Peachtree avoiding abandoned cars that littered the roadway. He encountered light traffic along the route as more and more cars were being freed from the icy traffic jam that had gripped the entire city. Within an hour, he had made his way to Roswell Road. Within another hour, he had reached downtown Alpharetta. Main Street looked almost like a Norman Rockwell painting with everything covered in snow. The streets of downtown were clear without any abandoned cars to mention. He proceeded North through town, and just outside of town, he hung a left. Around a curve and down a hill familiar horse farms came into his view. Everything around him was still and quiet, and covered in a blanket of white. A few more miles and he turned left into his subdivision. Several blocks later, he steered the pickup into the driveway and up the hill to the house.

A snow man greeted him on the front lawn sporting a multicolored scarf, two charcoal briquette eyes, a carrot nose, what appeared to be Skittles candies formed his smile, and one of John's cowboy hats.

"Someone's been having some fun," he said out loud.

As he followed the walkway from the driveway to the front porch, he stopped and noticed a wide packed path down the hill into the side yard. It only took a moment for him to recognize what he was seeing. Then he saw the round trashcan lid sitting at the bottom of the hill. The kids had discovered trashcan-lid sledding.

When he opened the front door, he was immediately greeted by Zeke, a 35-pound Bassett Hound with long droopy eyes and a wagging tail.

"Hey buddy," John said bending down to rub behind the dog's ears.

"DADDY!" came a yell from the kitchen and two sets of drumming feet before both children grabbed his legs. Mary followed them into the den.

"Welcome home, stranger," she said with a grin.

John laughed and embraced her with two children still firmly grabbing both of his legs.

"I'm betting you're starved. There is Brunswick Stew in the crock pot, and the kids have been making cookies. Don't be alarmed, the kitchen has not been bombed - just two small children who are a little messy," she reported.

John sat down on the hallway bench and pulled off his cowboy boots. He stood and pulled off his rancher coat and hung it on the coat rack. He walked into the kitchen, made himself a large bowl of stew, and sat down at the breakfast table at the edge of the kitchen. Mary carried two cups of coffee over and sat down at the table across from him as he ate. Between bites of stew, John relayed the story of the last 24 hours stuck on the interstate and the lady and baby he assisted. Mary listened intently while sipping coffee and bouncing one of their daughters on her knee. John rose and walked back to the crockpot for a second bowl of stew and then sat back down to eat it.

Mary began to tell him of the stories the local news had been reporting during the day - stories of complete strangers helping stranded drivers and stories of homeless forced to seek shelter and warmth. John listened and nodded while polishing off his second bowl of stew. Finally feeling full after the second bowl, he pushed himself back from the table a bit and began sipping his cup of coffee.

"You know," he began, "I've been thinking the last couple of days. When Uncle Herschel died, he left us that piece of land down near the speedway. He made a little money on the mobile home park and kept the taxes paid renting camping spots for the races on the rest of it. NASCAR only comes to the track once a year these days since they revamped their schedule. And I don't think the mobile home park rental business is all that lucrative. But if we sell all of that land, we are going to have one hell of a tax bill to pay. I'd really like to find a charity of some sort that could use some of that land for something useful and maybe donate a few acres to them."

Mary nodded in agreement. "Maybe Boy Scouts or a church would want land for camping or a retreat center," she said.

"Right," John replied, "and if we were to donate land, I would be inclined to donate the Mobile Home Park, because it already has electric, water, and septic on it. I think I am going to do a little talking around and see what we can figure out. It's a good hour's drive down there, and I really don't want to have to continue to manage that whole deal on top of my job. I think there are only four maybe five trailers rented out still. We can give those renters non-renewal notices, so they can begin figuring out where they are going to move while we figure out the rest."

"Sounds like a plan," Mary said in agreement. "I'm going to get these two in the bath and ready for bed. It's been a long eventful day."

As Mary herded the children upstairs for baths, John cleaned up the dishes from dinner and loaded the dishwasher. Zeke sat quietly a few feet behind him watching his every move.

"Zeke Ol' boy," John said as he finished loading the dishwasher and starting it's wash cycle, "you about ready for a walk?"

Zeke's tail began to pound the floor. He sprung up on all four feet and lumbered for the doorway, stopping at the coat rack where his leash hung and began nudging the end of the leash with his nose. John laughed at the sight.

"I'm gonna take that as a yes," John said.

He pulled his boots back on, put on his coat, and grabbed the leash. Zeke jumped up on his legs making it easy to attach the leash to his collar. The second the latch clicked, Zeke jumped back down and quickly tugged John to the door. John opened the door and Zeke led him out for their evening walk.

Chapter 14

Samuel Matthews set quietly behind the desk in his study pecking on the keyboard of the computer. He scrolled through the results of a Google search and clicked a link and then another. He sat for of a couple of hours reading article after article about the master-planned community being developed in Texas. As he read, Sam scribbled notes into a journal he had sitting beside the keyboard. After several hours, he had written four pages of notes. The more he read and wrote, the more his head was spinning with ideas. He knew he needed someone with business acumen to review what he was reading and discuss the viability of something similar being developed in the Metro Atlanta area. While having over half a decade of experience serving and pastoring, he knew he did not have the experience to even begin to plan something so complex and far reaching.

Sam pulled out his old flip style cell phone and dialed Phil Portman. Phil answered on the second ring.

"Hello?" Phil answered.

"Phil, this is Samuel Matthews," said Sam.

"Good morning, Sam," Phil replied, "What's got you stirring at 7am?"

Sam looked up at the clock on the study wall. He had not even realized what time it was or even what day of the week it was for that matter. He had sat at the hospital for so long that he had lost track of it all. He glanced down at the computer screen and saw the date. He moved the mouse over it to see that it was a Wednesday. He quickly tried to regain his composure and continue his phone conversation.

After what seemed to Phil as an unusually long pause, Sam continued; "Phil, I have been doing some research on something someone mentioned to me at the hospital this week. I would like you to do some reading and then let's get together and compare thoughts."

Phil responded without hesitation, "Sure Sam. What have you found?"

"A planned community for the chronically homeless. Not a shelter, but a planned community with travel trailers, mobile homes, and tiny houses. A place where the chronically homeless can receive medical attention, attend addiction rehabilitation, and where each person has their own home," Sam explained.

"Whoa!"Phil exclaimed, "That is a radical departure from the current solutions. Does such a place currently exist somewhere?"

Sam smiled, "Yes, such a place exists - just outside of Austin, Texas," he replied.

Phil's interest was piqued. He did not have any notions of cost or complexity. He was just filled with curiosity at the approach. He had seen shows on television from time to time about young people who were forgoing traditional housing to buy or build a tiny house that they could set in someone's backyard or could use for travelling. The idea of a homeless person living in one seemed like a genius solution compared to the old shelter approach.

From talking to the homeless that had sought shelter at Peachtree Church during the storm, Phil had learned of the pitfalls of the shelters. Anytime a large number of people with disabilities or addictions are housed in one large facility for long periods of time, it seemed to breed conflict. Several individuals he had talked with told of wanting personal space and security. Some avoided the shelters because of physical abuse and theft. Others just wanted space the shelters simply could not provide.

"Sam," he said; "Give me the name of the place and let me start reading."

Sam beamed, "Community First! Village," he replied.

"Thanks, Sam," he responded. "I am going to get studying up on this and I will give you a call when I am ready to discuss."

"Sounds great," Sam said.

Sam hung up the phone and looked around the study. He had not been home in a couple of days and a hot shower sounded like good medicine to him. He pushed himself back from the computer and slowly stood to his feet as his joints popped and creaked. He locked the study door behind him as he stepped into the hallway and then shuffled his way to the door leading outside to where his old tired Ford Crown Victoria sat waiting.

The driver's door creaked when Sam opened it as if to remind him how tired the old car was. He slowly slid behind the wheel and closed the door to another series of creaks. He put the key in the ignition switch and turned it. Nothing happened. He grabbed the shifter and rocked it between Park and Reverse a few times and tried again. But the old tired Crown Vic refused to wake from its slumber.

"Now isn't the time for this," Sam said out loud.

He pulled the key out of the ignition switch. He then slid the key right back into the switch. He rocked the gearshift between Park and Reverse a couple dozen times and then turned the key. The lights on the dash panel lit up, the starter slowly turned a few deliberate chugs, and then the old car fired to life.

Sam pulled the shifter into drive and the car made the familiar chug-chug-chug sound as it pulled out of the church parking lot and Sam headed home. Shortly, Sam rounded the corner and into the apartment building parking. He sought out a parking spot where the old Crown Vic would be faced out in the event it would not start and would need a tow or a jumpstart. One could not be too cautious with these old cars, he reasoned.

Two tugs on the interior door handle convinced the door to unlatch, and it creaked as Sam pushed it open. As he crawled out of the car and stood up, Sam was almost sure his hips and knees made as much noise as the door on the car. He gave the door a solid shove to close it. When it latched, rust fell from the bottom of the door.

Sam quietly shuffled towards his apartment. Slowly he ascended the stairway to the door of his unit. He opened the door, flung his coat and scarf onto a wingback chair sitting just inside the doorway and sat down to remove his shoes. His feet ached as he pulled off the shoes, so he paused and gently flexed his feet to try and relieve the pain.

After a moment, he rose to his feet and shuffled to his bedroom. He walked into the bathroom and turned on the hot water in the shower to give it time to heat up. He walked back into the bedroom and pulled a pair of flannel pajamas out of the dresser and laid them on the edge of the bed. He disrobed and tossed his clothes into a waiting hamper just outside the bathroom door. He shuffled back into the bathroom, adjusted the water temperature and then eased himself into the shower.

Sam stood under the warm water motionless for several minutes allowing the warmth of the water to soothe his aching joints and feet. Winter seemed to be just a little more difficult to withstand every year and a hot shower seemed to be the only solution for him. After a few minutes of hot water therapy, he shampooed what remained of his gray hair and then lathered his body in soap. After rinsing all the shampoo out of his hair and soap from his body, Sam again stood motionless under the hot water.

Finally, he turned the water off, pulled a thick towel off a hook on the wall, and began to dry himself. Wincing as he attempted to dry his lower legs and feet and he then sat on a shower stool for a moment for some relief, he shuffled out of the shower and across the bathroom stopping briefly to catch a glimpse of the tired figure in the mirror.

"Better give that old face a shave in the morning," he noted to himself.

He shuffled back to the bedroom and pulled on the flannel pajamas that he had laid out. He walked to the dresser across the room and retrieved his daily medication. He had missed a couple days' doses with the events of the week, so he wanted to make sure to take them before he retired for the night. He shuffled to the kitchen and poured himself a small glass of water from a pitcher in the refrigerator. He took the handful of pills in three segments to prevent choking. Then he finished off the glass of water for good measure. He set the glass in the sink, took a casual glance around the kitchen and living room, and then retired to his bedroom for a long overdue night of sleep.

Chapter 15

When Sam awoke on Saturday morning, he knew he needed to prepare a sermon for Sunday. He could not remember the last time he had gotten to Saturday without having already prepared a message. He shuffled into the kitchen and started a pot of coffee. He firmly believed nothing good had ever been accomplished without coffee. Once the coffee was ready, he poured himself a mug and sat down in one of the wingback chairs in the living room. He drew a long sip of coffee before setting it on the table beside the chair and retrieved a tablet and pen. Without much effort, he wrote across the top of the page, *"For God sent not his Son into the world to condemn the world; but that the world through him might be saved." - John 3:17.*

He sat and looked at those words on the page. For years, Sunday School teachers had taught children the verse just before it and even required they commit it to memory, but how many had read on to verse 17? Yes, John 3:16 proclaimed the Good News that God has loved the world so much that he sent his Son to pay the price for their sin and died in their place as an eternal sacrifice for all, but the following verse iced the cake as Sam liked to call it. For years, people struggled feeling condemned and unworthy of the love of a Savior, but God had removed all of that condemnation.

Sam's pen began to fly across the page, pausing briefly for him to take a couple longs sips of coffee and then continuing. At the end of the fifth page, Sam laid the pen down and began to read his draft while drinking the remaining coffee from the mug. Halfway through the reading, the mug went dry. Sam laid pages down on the table beside the chair and shuffled back to the coffee maker to replenish the mug. He drew a sip of the piping hot coffee and returned to his chair. He lifted the pages, and resumed reading. When he had completed his review, he tucked the pages inside his weathered Bible - ready for Sunday.

Sam picked up the remote control for the television, pushed a button and the television came to life. He pushed another button a few times until the

Atlanta Braves baseball game came into view. He settled into the comfort and support of the chair and began watching the game.

About the third inning, Sam's cellphone rang. He flipped it open and answered the call.

"Hello?"

"Sam," the voice said, "It's Phil."

"Well good morning to ya, Phil," Sam replied.

"Good afternoon, Sam;" Phil responded, noting it was going on two in the afternoon, "Clear your calendar for the week and pack a suitcase. I have two airline tickets for you and I to fly to Austin Monday and check out this homeless community you were talking about Friday."

Sam was almost dumbfounded, "Really?"

Phil smiled, "Yes really," he continued, "I did a lot of reading like you asked and was intrigued. So, I gave them a call. They have a kind of bed and breakfast arrangement where we can stay on the grounds and see how things all work first hand. So I went ahead and booked us both a flight for Monday to go take a look at things. I'll pick you up at 6AM Monday, and we will head to the airport."

"Alright," Sam said, "I better start getting things ready."

"Sounds good Sam," Phil replied, "See you in the morning."

Sam pushed a button on the phone to disconnect the call, closed the phone, returned it to his shirt pocket and returned his attention to the baseball game. At the end of the inning, he shuffled into the kitchen, made himself a sandwich, and poured himself another mug of coffee before returning to his chair and the baseball game.

As he watched the game, Sam considered how much the city of Atlanta had changed over the years. He remembered going to Braves baseball games at Fulton County Stadium for years when he was in college. But the old stadium had been demolished for the Olympics and was replaced by a more modern facility dubbed "the Ted" for Ted Turner who owned the Braves and TBS television network at the time. But this year, the Braves had moved to the North side of town into a newer even more modern park. As he thought about the changes with the baseball stadium, he drew a parallel to Peachtree Street Church. When he became the pastor at the church, it was a thriving center of the community with hundreds of families attending each week. These days they did not see 100 attend at Easter or Christmas - the two biggest church days of the year. Times were changing all around the midtown and downtown communities, and he knew things were going to have to change at Peachtree Street Church.

Chapter 16

Sunday came and went for Sam as hundreds of Sundays had over his 40 plus years as the Senior Pastor at Peachtree Street Church. He dutifully delivered the well-prepared message to the group of 35 or 40 people who sparsely populated the pews in the old sanctuary. At the conclusion of the morning worship service, he stood in the narthex – or what the general population might call the lobby – he shook hands, and smiled as the small group filed out of the sanctuary and out into the streets of midtown Atlanta.

Sam wondered to himself how long he would continue. He was past the age of retirement, and the diminishing congregation made him wonder if his work here was concluding. The board seemed dead set against selling the property despite numerous and lucrative offers. But, he knew that if they wanted to continue, the church would at some point need to find a new pastor. Lately, that someday seemed to be quickly approaching for Sam. Every day that he ascended the stairs to the sanctuary from the street or the stairs to his study, his joints would remind him that their willingness was diminishing.

As Sam and a couple of remaining volunteers locked the doors and secured the building, Sam thought that in the not too distant future he needed to initiate a difficult conversation with Phil Portman, the chairman of the Board of Trustees regarding his retirement. The board would have to make the decisions on the trajectory of the church after his retirement. Sam knew that time was quickly at hand, and he was at peace with it.

Sam shuffled out to the old Crown Vic, managed to get it started, and pointed it to Mary Mac's for his traditional Sunday afternoon lunch.

Chapter 17

It was early Monday morning when Phil pulled into the parking lot of Sam's apartment and parked his car. A few spaces over, he noted the presence of the old tired Ford LTD Crown Victoria that he recognized as Sam's. The faded paint, the one missing hubcap, and the crack at the base of the windshield all hinted at how tired the old car actually was. Phil was amazed that it still started and drove. As he walked to the door of Sam's apartment, Phil found himself drawing a comparison of the old Crown Vic and Sam. Both were weathered and tired and both were still going after years of service.

Phil knocked on the door. He could hear what he thought was a shuffling sound. After a few minutes, he could hear the sound of several mechanisms being unlocked and the door opened to Sam dressed in a pair of khakis, button down shirt, and a sports coat.

"Good morning, Phil," Sam said with a smile.

"Morning, Sam," Phil replied; "Are you ready for this adventure?"

"As ready as I can be,", Sam responded. "I'll warn you now that I may slow you down on the walking. I'm not the spring chicken I once was. In fact, I'm carrying my cane along with us. I try not to use it around the church much unless I am having a really rough day. I don't want the congregation worrying. But for getting through the airports and such, I figure it's in my best interest."

"Absolutely," Phil quickly replied, "and we can get some assistance from the airlines as well. No need to kill yourself getting through the airport. You need to save your strength for the destination."

Sam turned and pulled a rolling suitcase to the door. He retrieved his weathered Bible from the table beside his chair and looked up at Phil.

"Well, I think I have everything I need," he said.

"Let me get that bag for you," Phil said, reaching past Sam for the suitcase.

"Thank you," Sam responded.

He closed the door to the apartment behind them, pulled out a ring of keys and secured three locks. And the two proceeded to the parking lot - Phil rolling the suitcase along with Sam a bit slower aided by his cane following. When they reached Phil's Mercedes, he opened the truck and stowed Sam's suitcase beside his. He darted around to the passenger door and opened it as Sam was approaching. Sam slid into the seat, laid his cane against the seat and fastened his seat belt, then closed the car door. Phil retreated to the driver side, crawled in, and started the car.

"If you want some relief for your back, this car has heated seats," Phil said.

"Oh, that would probably be a good idea," Sam said.

Phil reached over and pushed a button.

"I'm setting it on low," he explained, "If you want it warmer, just push this button again. It has three heat settings."

"Thank you," Sam replied.

Phil put the car in gear and headed for the interstate and began the route to the airport. He had driven it many times and drove it more from memory than anything. As they drove, Sam figured now was as good as any time to start the difficult conversation that he had been putting off for a couple of years.

"Phil," he began, "I've given it a lot of thought and I believe I am going to retire from serving as the Senior Pastor at the end of the year."

While somewhat stunned, Phil had known it was something that was on the horizon. He glanced over at Sam.

"What was the final factor, the dwindling attendance or your mobility?" Phil asked.

Sam chuckled. "A combination of those factors and a few others actually," he responded to the question.

"I can understand," Phil said, "The board has not put any plan together for contingency, so it's good you're providing 11 months for us to chart a course."

Sam smiled, "Precisely my line of thinking."

"Have you decided where you are going or what you are going to do yet?" Phil inquired.

"No," Sam replied, "I am going to be trying to figure that one out over the next several months as well."

"Well, I would say we all have a lot of decisions and planning to do over the course of this year," Phil noted. "So regarding today's business, I really like this model they have implemented in Austin. Apparently they initially tried to launch it a couple of times within the city limits, but they encountered resistance from neighbors at a couple potential sites and the obligatory zoning regulations. So they settled on a site in the unincorporated area in the county just outside of Austin where they were not encumbered by all of the zoning and other technicalities. They have a mixture of travel trailers, RVs, and tiny houses so that each resident has his or her own home that provides for their privacy and dignity. They have created a facility that serves as a sort of clinic where doctors, dentists, as well as social workers and lawyers can visit and provide pro bono services."

Sam nodded while he talked, listening intently to every detail. "You know, with the amount of homeless veterans and homeless that are elderly, that sounds like an ideal environment for someone that is self sufficient and does not need to be in a nursing home or such. The more I think about it, it even sounds like a place that could use a retired minister to live on property," he said.

Phil quickly glanced over at Sam. "I had not given that a thought, but you have a good point. If we had something like that in the Atlanta area, it might be a pretty good place for a retired minister who did not want to completely unplug from ministry.," he noted.

Soon, Sam started noticing aircraft lights in the sky above them. A few minutes later and they were arriving at the airport. Phil drove them to covered parking that was the closest to the terminal opting to pay for the convenience of getting Sam as close to the main terminal as possible without dropping him at the door.

Phil pulled out his phone and snapped a shot of the parking sign near the car to make it easy to remember the aisle and section where they parked on their return. He then opened the trunk, retrieved their two roller bags and his laptop bag. He latched his laptop bag to his roller bag and began rolling the two behind him.

"I can pull mine along, Phil," Sam said.

"It's not a problem Sam," I can handle them both with ease," Phil replied, refusing to relinquish the bag.

"Alright," Sam conceded, "Thank you."

"My pleasure, my friend," Phil replied. "I am going to get the airlines to get you a roller chair so you don't wear yourself out walking thru this airport. I want you rested and able to walk around when we get to Austin."

Sam started to protest, but Phil stopped him. "I know you can walk and don't need a wheel chair. But if you walk the length of this airport and aggravate your back and joints, you will be sitting in the middle of a large tract of land outside Austin and unable to get around. So, why don't we go with a roller chair in the airport and save your energy for where it's important?"

Sam relented, "Alright."

Phil guided them to security and after several minutes of what Sam thought felt like a cattle drive weaving through mazes of lines, the two maneuvered through security and headed down a long escalator to the transportation tunnel. They boarded a train and headed for their concourse. Four stops later, they exited the tram and walked across to another long escalator that took them up to the concourse where they would be catching their flight. Phil guided them to a customer service counter and requested a roller chair for Sam. After a few minutes, a Sky Cap appeared with a chair. Sam eased himself into the chair and sat quietly as they proceeded to their gate at the other end of the concourse. Once at the gate, Sam thanked the Sky Cap and moved to one of the seats at the gate. Phil palmed the Sky Cap a twenty dollar bill and thanked him for his service.

"Sam," Phil called out, "I'm going to walk over to Starbucks for a coffee. Can I get you something?"

"I never turn down coffee," Sam replied with a grin.

"Anything in it?"

"No," Sam answered, "just black coffee."

Phil returned shortly with two large cups and handed one to Sam. "I got my usual Flat White. I got you a Blonde Roast. Hope it's to your liking," he said.

"Thanks," Sam replied; "I'm sure it's fine."

While the two sipped their coffees, Phil pulled out his laptop and quietly began working on something. Sam, a natural student of human nature, watched the people moving around the airport with great interest. The Atlanta airport was a gateway for international flights entering the United States, so there were people of all nationalities. He saw hair of every color in the big box of Crayola crayons and clothing of every style from current to 50 years ago.

After another 30-45 minutes, the airline gate agent made a call for early boarding for passengers needing assistance or a little extra time for boarding. Sam knew this was his call. With the aid of his cane, he slowly rose to his feet. Phil stowed the laptop back in his bag and retrieved their boarding passes and followed him to the gate attendant. He handed her

Sam's boarding pass and then his. He then followed Sam aboard with the two bags in tow.

When they arrived to their seats, Sam was surprised to see Phil had purchased them both first class seats. He was grateful for Phil's generosity knowing the seats would be more spacious and comfortable. Sam slid into his assigned seat, and Phil stowed their bags in the overhead. He then slid into the seat beside Sam.

"This is some pretty expensive seating," Sam quietly noted to Phil.

Phil smiled, "Perks, my friend, from all of my international travel. I have been saving up flier miles and have not ever used them. This seemed like a good use," he said.

Sam nodded, "Well thank you. It's very generous of you," he replied.

Once the flight was airborne, the flight attendants served the first class cabin breakfast. Once Phil finished eating, He retrieved his laptop and began working again. Sam admired the man's work ethic and wondered if he ever rested or relaxed. He did not inquire to what he was working on, he instead pulled out his Bible and began to read.

When the flight landed in Austin, another Sky Cap was waiting to greet them when they stepped off the plane into the jetway. Sam slid into the chair and laid his bible and cane across his lap. Phil followed them with the two bags in tow. They crossed the airport making their way to the rental car pickup area. Phil had a large SUV waiting for them when they arrived. Again he palmed the Sky Cap a twenty dollar bill while Sam was not looking and thanked him for his service. He stowed their bags in the back of the vehicle while Sam climbed into the passenger side.

Phil climbed in under the steering wheel and started the vehicle.

"Oh look," Sam exclaimed, "heated seats!"

He pushed the button on his side and settled in for their drive. Phil smiled and pushed the button on his side as well. He pulled the vehicle into gear and navigated for the exit. He pulled his smartphone from his pocket and made a couple of selections and then laid the phone on the console between them. Sam looked down to see an animated road map. A voice began providing them directions to their destination. Sam chuckled at the thought. His flip phone did not provide that functionality.

Soon they were on a Texas highway. Sam was amazed at the stark difference in the landscape here in Texas compared to Georgia. Lush green was replaced by the shades of red and tans and there was an absence of the abundant trees to which he was accustomed. Phil maneuvered the twisting roads without a word while Sam gazed out the windows focusing on older buildings and the rolling hills in the distance.

Following the guidance of the voice on his cell phone, Phil made a turn onto a smaller country road. Sam looked up in time to see a solitary road sign. "Hog Eye Road" the sign read. Sam smiled as he thought to himself, it doesn't get more country than Hog Eye Road. He continued to take in the countryside around them - an old weathered barn leaning to one side surrounded by a well weather worn fence constructed of mesquite fence posts and barbed wire. Further down, the road began to bend and Sam could see a village begin to appear. As they descend a hill and pass through open gates, Sam could see little houses scattered across the property. Some were metal structures with modern design, others were traditional wood frames with screened porches, while even others were travel trailers and RVs.

Phil pulled the vehicle to a stop and put it in park. They both sat motionless for a few minutes simply soaking in their surroundings. They both looked up and saw a figure slowly approaching them - a grey haired bearded man with a toothy grin wearing a baseball cap. Phil rolled down the window on the driver's side and greeted him, "Good Morning," he called out.

The man walked to the window, stretched out his arm and responds, "Good morning, welcome to Community First! Village. My name is Dominic."

"I'm Phil," Phil responded shaking the man's hand, "and this is Reverend Samuel Matthews."

"Just call me Sam," Sam quickly interjected.

"Would y'all like the 50 cent tour?" Dominic asked.

"You bet!" Sam exclaimed.

Phil shut off the engine of the SUV and both men climbed out - Sam shuffling with his cane. Dominic led them to the Bed and Breakfast composed of tall teepees and shiny Airstream travel trailers.

"You boys will be sleeping in one of our Airstreams while you are here. We didn't think Sam's joints would withstand sleeping in a teepee for a couple of nights," he said as they both quietly surveyed their surroundings.

He then led them to the amphitheater and fire pit.

"A lot of community is created here," he continued; "We hold a summer film festival and invite families to visit with us. On cooler nights we light up a fire in the fire pit, roast some weenies, make some s'mores, and play guitars. It's a really good place for community gathering and fellowship, and it's a great place for neighbors to get to know each other."

After a few minutes, he led the two men to the Health Center building where mental care, health care, hospice, and respite care services are provided to residents of the community. The men were speechless in amazement at the level of care and services that were available. They saw the market and the hospitality center before wandering through the community farm complete with goats, chickens, bee hives, an aquaponic system raising catfish, fresh vegetable garden, as well as fruit trees and nut trees.

They then toured the blacksmith shop and the carpentry shop where classes are provided and items are created for sale. Their tour ended in the center of the village in a garden containing a huge chess set and playground surrounded by beautiful flowers.

Sam broke the silence. "It is breathtaking," he said, "I could never imagine this in all of my wildest dreams. I probably wouldn't believe it existed without seeing it with my own two eyes. I have spent most of my life wondering what it would have been like to live in the Garden of Eden. Now, I feel like I have actually experienced it myself firsthand."

Phil chimed in, "You know," he started, "Ever since the storm, things have really changed in my mind and life concerning the plight of the homeless. After spending two and a half days interacting with those in our community struggling with a place to call home, I have kept saying to myself 'there has to be a better way.' But I could not come up with a workable solution. I knew the shelters were not the ultimate solution for a variety of factors with the biggest being the inability to restore an individual's dignity. But y'all have done it here. Individuals have their own home. They have privacy they haven't had in years. They have personal space where they can sleep in peace without worrying about having their shoes stolen. They do not have to worry about where their next meal is coming from, because they can walk right out their front door and collect eggs or pick fruit or vegetables. They have ready access to health care. They can even learn a new skill or craft. But most importantly, they can feel a sense of community and belonging."

Dominic smiled as he listened to their observations, "You clearly see the vision, gentlemen. I believe that we are able to provide those who want it restored dignity, genuine community - where everyone knows your name and you feel like you belong, and the power and freedom of choice that they have not had for years."

Sam and Phil accepted an invitation to join other visitors and community residents for lunch at the Community Center. They sat down at the wooden tables elbow to elbow with complete strangers and enjoyed a completely organic meal prepared from food produced on the grounds. As they ate and visited with those at their tables, they were encouraged by the stories of the community residents. Many of their stories started much like the stories they heard during the two and a half days they provided shelter in the storm in Atlanta. But these stories changed. They did not end with the individuals walking out warm and with a full belly back into the cold Atlanta streets. These stories ended with individuals being awarded a RV or a tiny house, a sense of dignity, and a sense of community. They woke each morning knowing they were surrounded by people who cared and genuinely wanted good things for their lives.

Sam and Phil spent the remainder of the day visiting with members of the community, helping feed animals, helping cook dinner, carrying split firewood to the fire pit, and simply enjoying the community that existed. When they arrived back at the Airstream travel trailer that was their room at the Bed and Breakfast, Phil struggled to shut his mind down to be able to get to sleep. He finally gave up. He quietly crawled out of bed, walked to the other end of the Airstream and sat down at the sofa and pull out dining table. He retrieved his laptop and began typing away.

Unaware of how long he had been typing, Phil glanced down at the corner of the laptop screen and noticed it was 2 AM. He closed the laptop. Quietly walked back to the bedroom area, and crawled back into the bed. Within minutes he was sound asleep.

Chapter 18

John kissed his family goodbye and tossed his suitcase in the passenger side of his pickup. He crawled in and fired the truck to life. He took a long swig of coffee from his travel mug before dropping it in the cup holder in the console. He looked around and then backed the truck out of the driveway and headed for the airport. He had made the journey down Georgia 400 and I-75 to the airport, it almost seemed automatic to him. But this trip seemed different. He glanced out the side windows as he passed 14th Street and the area just South of it where he had spent the night with a total stranger and her baby in the cab of his truck during the winter storm.

In just over an hour, he was pulling into the parking deck and finding a parking spot. He shut the truck off, pulled out his cellphone, and noted his parking details in an app on the phone for future reference. He walked around the truck to the passenger side and took out his suitcase, set it on the ground next to the truck, and extended the handle. He threw his laptop bag over his shoulder, closed the truck door, and pressed a button on the keyfob to lock the truck. It responded with two quick chirps of the horn. He set off for the terminal at a fast paced walk with his roller bag in tow. Across the parking deck, down a ramp to the ground level, he made quick work to cross the roadway between the parking deck and the main terminal anxious to get out of the cold wind. When he stepped through the automatic doors into the terminal, he slowed his pace a bit and continued towards the queue line for security. While the crowd in front of him slowly snaked its way through the ribbon maze, he emptied his pockets into his laptop bag, retrieved his driver's license and boarding pass.

After about 15 minutes of the slow snaking queue line, he reached the TSA podium and presented the agent his driver's license and boarding pass. The agent slowly reviewed his license and then the boarding pass before making a mark on the boarding pass with a highlighter and returning it and his license to him. John looked up at 8 lines in front of him that all appeared congested, so he elected to try his luck by going to his right around to two other lines. Down a narrow corridor, he followed several other travelers and was pleased to find a small group in front of him proceeding at a decent pace. He grabbed a tray and placed his shoes and belt in it along with a bag containing toothpaste and other liquids and gels. He grabbed a second tray, pulled his laptop out of his laptop bag and placed it in a tray by itself. He placed the two trays, his suitcase, and laptop bag on the conveyor feeding an X-ray machine and then stepped towards a body scanner. He stopped and looked at a TSA agent who motioned for him to step into the scanner. He placed his feet in the outlines on the floor and held his hands up as if someone had said "stick 'em up." He stood motionless for several seconds until the agent told him to step through. He stepped out of the scanner onto a rubber mat where he waited and watched a red light in front of him. When the light turned green, he stepped forward to a conveyor belt and retrieved his laptop bag, suitcase, and the two trays he had prepared. He repacked the laptop into his laptop bag, stowed the bag of liquids and gels back in his suitcase, stepped into his shoes, threaded his belt back through his slacks, and put his other belongings back in his pockets. He stacked the two trays on top of a stack at the end of the conveyor and proceeded to the long escalators down to the transportation level.

Once at the bottom of the escalator, he began walking through the level bypassing the airport train system electing for a bit of exercise on his way to the concourse for his flight. After another 15 minutes of walking he arrived at the escalator up to the concourse and stepped on it, relaxing for a brief moment. When the escalator delivered him to the concourse, he stepped off, and headed down the concourse towards his gate. Halfway there he stopped at a Starbucks and purchased what he referred to as a "Cup of Inspiration." He began sipping his coffee as he headed to the gate. When he arrived at the gate, he checked the display above the gate agent's podium for the flight's estimated arrival and departure times which appeared unaltered indicating no delays. He then scanned the available seating and found an open seat near the podium, which he figured would help in boarding. He sat his laptop bag on top of his suitcase and sat down in the seat he had chosen and began enjoying his coffee. He checked his phone and responded to a few emails.

He had grown tired of all of the travel his job required, but at least this would be a short trip. He would meet with the leaders from a developer starting a new master planned community outside of Round Rock, Texas just North of Austin. The area had seen a great deal of growth over the years and a master planned community offered families neighborhood shopping and restaurants as well as schools, doctors, and dentists offices all within walking distance of their homes. Their meeting would last most of the day, he would spend the night and be on a flight home tomorrow - things could be worse he figured.

Half an hour had passed when John heard a noise and looked up to see a gate agent opening the door to the boarding ramp. Soon a wave of humanity began pouring from the boarding into the gate area. Several men in suits came off at a brisk pace and headed for the escalators. A college kid was next in a sweatshirt and a guitar bag slung over his shoulder. Another hundred or more people followed in step. Once the plane had emptied, the gate agent made an announcement that the crew was cleaning the plane, and they would begin boarding shortly. John checked his watch and to his surprise it appeared the flight might depart on time. A rarity, he figured, for the airline and for the busy Atlanta airport. He tossed his empty coffee cup in a nearby trashcan which initiated the sound of an electric motor for a brief moment. John figured it must be an automatic compactor.

Several minutes later, boarding began. John's frequent travel and first class ticket got him onboard quickly. He stowed his roller bag in the overhead, and his laptop under the seat. The flight attendant brought him coffee and a hot cloth and asked if he would like anything else to drink. John declined. After several minutes the steady line of passengers dwindled down and the flight attendant began the flight safety speech demonstrating how to buckle a seat belt. John wondered if there was anyone on the face of the earth that had ever boarded an airplane and did not have the rudimentary knowledge of how to fasten a seat belt. Heck his youngest buckled and unbuckled the harness all the time in the car seat. Did they really need to demonstrate this every flight? The seat belt demonstration was closely followed by the five exits of the plane, the lighting on the floor, and the demonstration of oxygen masks falling from the overhead with the reminder to put your own mask on before trying to help someone else.

John rolled his eyes and thought "Of course, because if you pass out due to lack of oxygen, you won't be able to help someone else."

This thrilling demonstration was followed by an explanation of how your seat cushion could be used for a floatation device. John wondered if anyone who had ever been in an emergency landing in water had to forgo using their seat cushion as a flotation device because it had been soiled on the landing.

Finally all of the flight attendant drama presentation concluded. One flight attendant walked the length of the plane ensuring all the overhead compartments were closed and latched. Two others walked the aisles to ensure everyone had figured out how to buckle their seat belt, had their seat in the upright position, their tray table stowed, and any items neatly tucked under the seat in front of them. One final check to ensure the door was securely latched and the flight attendants took their jump seats and gave one last demonstration of how one latches a seat belt.

A few minutes later the captain came on the public address system and thanked everyone for choosing this airline, gave a synopsis of how long the flight would take and where they were in line to taxi out to the runway. The ground crew pushed the plane back from the gate and then the flight crew took over. A few short engine revs and several stops and the aircraft was in line behind 10 or so more waiting for their turn on one of Atlanta's runways. After several more minutes the pilot reached the end of the taxi strip and began to turn the plane for the runway, stopping at a line on the asphalt while the aircraft in front of them accelerated and took flight. Finally it was their turn. The pilot rolled the aircraft onto the end of the runway and centered it on the dotted line. The aircraft sat motionless for a few minutes and then a sudden rev of the jet engines and they were underway. John considered that this must be what it felt like to launch a NHRA drag car off the line at the Atlanta Dragway. The nose of the aircraft began to lift and then the plane was in flight. John could hear the sound of hydraulics folding up the landing gear and wing flaps changing position.

After several more minutes, John heard the sound of a doorbell chime twice and the flight attendants unbuckled their seat belts and began working in the galley. Breakfast was served to the first class passengers and John was more than ready to eat. The flight attendant refilled his coffee mug that was emblazoned with the airlines logo on it and he began to enjoy his breakfast.

Chapter 19

Sam woke up several times during the night. As he got older, this was becoming the norm more than the exception. He made a couple of trips to the bathroom in the Airstream over the course of the night. When he woke up at 5 AM, he decided there was not much point in trying to get back to sleep again. So, he quietly arose, made the bed, changed out of his pajamas into the day's clothes, folded the pajamas and neatly put them back into his suitcase. He stepped into the bathroom, plugged in his electric razor and gave himself his daily shave. He washed his face, brushed his teeth, and combed what was left of his gray hair. He returned the toiletry to his suitcase, sat down in the swivel chair by the door and slowly put on his socks and shoes. This had become the slowest part of getting ready in the morning over the last couple of years. If he spent too long with a sock or tying a shoe, he would get breathless.

Once completely ready, he grabbed his cane from beside the door and used it to help himself get up from the swivel chair. He opened the door and carefully maneuvered down the two foldout steps and closed the trailer door. He began walking with no particular direction in mind, admiring the beauty of the different design of tiny houses scattered across the community. After a couple of minutes of walking, he came upon a sight he had not noticed yesterday. Nestled between several of the houses was a small chapel with a red door and a breathtaking stained glass image that Sam quickly recognized. It was the repentant criminal that was crucified next to Jesus. Sam could remember Jesus words to the man, "Today You shall be with Me in Paradise."

Sam walked around the little chapel paying painfully close attention to every detail. Once he had completely circled the building, he walked to the red door and reached his hand out for the knob. He was surprised to find it unlocked. For so many years they had been so careful to ensure all the doors were locked at Peachtree Street Church; it seemed odd but refreshing to him. He stepped inside the chapel and stood motionless, slowly eyeing every square inch of the interior of the chapel. After a while, his hips and knees started aching from standing so long so he found a place to sit. He sat in wonderment of everything he had seen over the last 24 hours at this incredible place. He bowed his head in silence and began to pray.

Back at the Airstream, Phil had awakened and realized Sam was nowhere to be found. He found it odd, but he was not alarmed. He elected to start his day with a shower in the trailer's small bathroom and then conducted his morning routine – shaving with a safety razor, brushing his teeth, combing his hair, and a dash of cologne for good measure. He dressed, and walked into the Airstream's galley kitchen where he eyed a coffee maker. In the cabinet just above it, he found filters, packs of coffee, and mugs. He prepped the coffee maker and turned it on to brew. He walked over to the fold out dining table and fired up his laptop while he waited for the coffee.

After several minutes of typing, the travel trailer was filled with the aroma of freshly made coffee. He poured himself a mug, sat back down in front of the laptop and continued his work.

Chapter 20

John awoke from a nap to two chimes that sounded like a doorbell. He opened his eyes and looked around to see that the flight attendants were busy collecting mugs and dishes from the first class passengers. The Captain's voice came over the public address system and told the passengers that the flight would be beginning its descent into the Austin area. He relayed the current weather conditions and estimated they would be touching down in 30 minutes. He concluded with the customary, seat belt light going on, no moving around the cabin, and other details that John had heard too many times previously.

A few minutes later, the lead flight attendant began her announcement of seats in the upright position, and tray tables stowed. John had heard it so many times, he halfway expected to hear them say "With every head bowed and every eye closed, we're gonna sing the last verse of Amazing Grace 6 more times." Like he had heard a hundred times in the Baptist church where he grew up. He reached across the empty seat beside him and opened the window shade and stared out at the vast rolling landscape beneath them and the occasional wisp of a cloud between. His mind wandered across hundreds of topics, but today's meeting was not one of them. He was confident that he was prepared to handle the discussions. Because he had previously planned all the details, he didn't have any concerns about what was coming No, the dominant recurring thought this morning was how to deal with Uncle Herschel' s land. Atlanta Motor Speedway had been reduced to one NASCAR event a year, and they had made acres of the speedway property open to campers. So the days of Uncle Herschel renting out part of the land to fans camping a few miles down the road were over. The mobile home park tenants were almost completely gone. With his work schedule, his time with his family was precious and he would much rather spend time with his wife and children when he was home than worry with mowing that piece of land.

Looking out the window, John could tell they were now on their final approach. He set back up in his seat, planted his feet directly on the floor, and crossed his arms. This was something he had done so many times he did not even think about it anymore. But years ago he had learned that most airline crashes happen on takeoff and landing. And he had learned that the majority of people who died in crash landings died due to flail injuries, or broken feet where they could not get up and get out after the crash. Broken feet occurred because passengers had their feet under the seat in front of them and on a hard impact the seats collapsed on their feet. So now out of habit, John had assumed the defensive takeoff and landing position without giving it so much as a thought.

He heard the landing gear drop into position, and he heard the hydraulics setting the wing flaps. Within minutes he felt the rear wheels touchdown and he immediately heard the pilot reverse the engine thrust as he quickly slowed the plane. The front gear touched down, and then he heard the braking.

"Welcome to Austin, the live music capital of the world!" The captain began his final address on the public address system. He chattered away about what gate they would be arriving at and how they knew the passengers had a myriad of choices in air travel and they appreciated them selecting this airline. John wondered if there was any sincerity in that whole speech or if it was as meaningless reciting it as it was to repeatedly hearing it.

When the door opened, he stepped into the aisle, grabbed his laptop bag and tossed it over his shoulder, and retrieved his suitcase from the overhead. He extended the handle and rolled it along behind him as he walked off the plane and up the jetway to the terminal. Once inside the terminal, he turned and headed for the ground transportation. He walked by numerous shops selling books and magazines and Keep Austin Weird shirts, hats, and mugs before reaching the ground transportation area. As he walked out of the secured area of the terminal into the ground transportation area, he spotted a middle-aged man in a black suit holding a small whiteboard with his last name on it. He walked directly to the man.

"Hi," he said, "I'm John."

"Good Morning, Sir," the man replied, "My name is Randall. I will be driving you to the company's headquarters. Allow me to get your bags."

"Thanks," John replied, handing over the roller bag. "I'm good with the laptop bag."

Randall led him out of the terminal to a waiting black SUV. He opened the rear door for John and then headed to the rear of the vehicle where he loaded his suitcase. Randall walked briskly around to the driver's door and crawled in under the steering wheel.

"You picked a good day to visit Austin," Randall said, as he started the SUV and pulled it into gear. "No rain on the radar and mild temperatures."

"Awesome," John replied.

Randall turned on some jazz music on the stereo, pulled the SUV onto the Interstate and headed for Round Rock. John pulled out his phone and sent a quick text to his wife, "On the ground in Austin, heading for Round Rock. Hope you have a wonderful day. I love you."

He scanned a few emails on his phone and then slid it back into his pocket. Lying in the seat beside him was a copy of USA Today, so he picked it up and began reading.

Chapter 21

After a couple of hours at the keyboard of the laptop, Phil looked down at the corner of the screen and noticed it was almost 11 AM. He stretched, stood up, set the coffee mug in the sink, turned off the coffee maker, and decided to find Sam. He slid on a pair of tassel loafers and stepped out of the Airstream. Closing the door behind him, he pondered momentarily which direction to head. He finally decided on a direction and set off walking. He checked the hospitality center, the community market, the garden, the dog park, the amphitheater, but to no avail. After almost an hour of wandering, he saw a sight that drew his attention - a small chapel. He did not recall seeing it the day before, but then again, they had seen a great deal in one day. He was suddenly certain he knew where Sam was. He increased his pace toward the chapel. When he reached the red front door, he quietly opened it and stepped inside. There he found Sam seated with his head bowed, silent, and motionless. He quietly put his hand on Sam's shoulder. Sam opened his eyes and glanced upward.

"Well," he said, "Good morning, Phil."

"Good Morning," Phil replied; " Been here all morning?"

Sam chuckled. "Yes, I have," he said, "For the life of me I couldn't tell you for how long."

Phil smiled, "If I were forced to guess," he said, "I'd say about five hours."

Sam furrowed his brows, "Seriously?"

"Seriously," Phil replied. "I've been up a little over three hours, and you were long gone when I awoke."

Sam nodded. "Well yeah," he said somewhat sheepishly. "My internal alarm doesn't seem to let me sleep past 6 anymore it seems. I've quitting fretting it or fighting against it. I have resigned to just get up and get on with my day."

"Are you hungry?" Phil asked.

"Now that you mention it," Sam replied, "I am."

Phil smiled, "Well you are in luck," he said. "The community center has some sandwiches and fruit they were setting out when I was by there a few minutes ago."

Sam reached for his cane. "I guess we better get a move on then," he said with a grin.

The two men walked across the grounds back to the community center.

"I see why you insisted on the roller chair in the airport. This place is huge. There is a lot of walking around here," Sam commented.

"They have a couple of golf carts if you get needing one," Phil said. " But I thought if I could convince you to save your energy at the airport that you would probably enjoy strolling around this community."

"I really have," Sam replied, "I have been thinking all night that this is the kind of place I could retire, enjoy, and feel useful. We need to find a way to do something like this in Atlanta."

Phil smiled. "How did I know you were thinking that?"

"Probably because you are thinking the same thing," Sam responded.

"Guilty," Phil exclaimed. "I just keep thinking that we have so many homeless veterans and elderly in Atlanta that would enjoy a place like this and it is such an improvement over the shelter model. Nothing against the shelters, but they are a temporary solution. Transitional at best. This is a sustainable model - a permanent solution to address several underlying issues instead of just addressing shelter."

Sam nodded in agreement, "But the magnitude of a project this scale and the money it must cost to complete it is staggering," he said.

Phil shook his head, "I completely agree with you", he said, "It's not a project one church or four or five people can complete. It would take a community - corporate sponsors, churches, civic groups, doctors, dentists, lawyers, and other volunteers working together. We would have to clearly define the vision, and begin pitching it to other churches, civic groups, and businesses and ask them to partner with us. But think about it, Sam. We have the corporate headquarters of Home Depot in Atlanta as well as the corporate headquarters for hundreds of other companies. And some of us are fortunate enough to rub elbows with some of those CEOs at lunch in Mary Macs, in Lions Club meetings, on the golf courses. You might be surprised at some of the contacts some of the board members at the church have."

Sam stopped walking and looked up at Phil. "What you are saying is, you think it could be done."

Phil looked Sam straight in the eyes. "There is not a doubt in my mind. I have already made a list of folks that I have contact with that I want to talk to when we get back," Phil said, "And I've been working on some ideas on what we need and what a sponsorship for each building or service might look like. We're just going to have to find some land outside the city. Somewhere that is not strangled in zoning and subdivisions that would fight something like this. Dominic told me that they tried to launch on two or three other tracts of land and constantly encountered resistance before landing on this property."

Sam resumed walking towards the community center.

"I would say we have a good deal of work ahead of us," he said as he walked; "and in a little over 10 months, I can be there, wherever there is, fulltime."

The two reached the community center and walked into the shared kitchen where they found a couple trays of freshly picked fruit and a tray of sandwiches. They both filled a plate and grabbed a bottle of water before walking out to one of the wooden tables where they sat down to eat.

"You know," Phil said between bites, "we are going to need someone with experience at developing a master plan for something of this scale. Because you cannot build it all at once, so you need a master plan to map out where everything will be once it is completed, then you can build it in phases."

Sam silently nodded as he listened and ate.

Chapter 22

Randall pulled the SUV into the circular driveway and up to the tall glass front doors of the tallest building in the office park and put the vehicle in park. John let himself out before Randall could get the door for him, so he continued on around the vehicle, opened the rear door, and retrieved John's bag for him.

"Thank you, Sir," John said.

"Don't mention it, Sir," Randall replied.

John gave him a twenty dollar bill as Randall handed him the bag. He turned and headed in the doors, across the marble lined lobby, and to the elevators. He paused for a moment at the directory and confirmed the floor before punching the elevator call button. Within a couple of minutes, the elevator door opened, and he pushed the button for the 12th floor.

"Going up," John said to no one, "Penthouse suite."

He watched the numbers change on the digital display above the button panel as the elevator passed the other 11 floors. When the display showed 12, he said "Yahtzee!"

When the elevator doors opened and he stepped off, he was immediately greeted by one of the district managers for the firm.

"Hello, John," the man said, "How was your flight?"

"Pleasantly uneventful," John said with a chuckle.

The man grinned, "Well that is always good," he said.

He led John to a conference room surrounded by glass windows. Six people were gathered around the table when he walked in the room. They all stopped mid-conversation to greet him. He headed for an empty chair and sat down at the table. At the head of the table was the Senior Vice President of the development company, Dennis Smith.

"Alright, looks like everyone is here. Let's take a final look at the revised master plan," he said as he clicked the mouse on his laptop and a multicolored map appeared on a screen at the end of the room.

"So," John started, "let's begin at the front entrance and work our way through the grounds. As you enter from the highway, you turn onto a brick paved drive that circles a large fountain. Once you pass the fountain, you arrive at the community main square. The main square is composed of three story buildings with shops on the first level with curbside parking and loft apartments on the second and third levels. At the far end of the square sits a single story restaurant with a parking lot to its rear. Just past the square lies a series of one story and two story buildings with space for restaurants, bars, an ice cream shop, and a bakery. Just beyond the bakery on the right side is a three story parking deck. To the left side of the roadway is an amphitheatre. Further down the road lies a jogging trail and dog park; and behind those are soccer fields, softball fields, and football fields. Across the road from the sports fields there are three buildings separated by a large circular driveway. This is an elementary, middle, and high school with a gymnasium behind each building. Adjacent to the sports fields is a large two-story field house that will house the YMCA. The road then bends to the right and connects to four gated subdivisions. The first one to the right contains lots for 1,100 townhomes with one-car garages. The first one to the left contains lots for 1,600 one-story homes ranging from 1,100 to 1,500 square feet. The next one on the right contains lots for 1,800 two-story homes ranging from 1,850 to 2,300 square feet and two car garages. The final one on the left contains 3,020 lots for two to three story homes ranging from 3,000 - 4,800 square feet. Just past the entrance of the last subdivision is a three bay fire station. The road way bends around the rear of the property providing access to the highway both North of the development and South of the development without requiring to drive through the community square."

A discussion followed with everyone at the table asking questions and John answering them and detailing items on the map. One by one, he answered every question to the satisfaction of the requestor. Dennis sat at the head of the table admiring John's command of the room. Everyone had input on the original design and every tweak John had made to the design over the last six months. His attention to everyone's concerns and his attention to detail was noticed and appreciated. When the last question was answered, a young woman opened the door of the conference room and wheeled in a cart with boxed lunches. John had not even noticed the time, but he welcomed the break. A hush fell over the room as everyone concentrated on eating. John recalled as a child one summer a revival preacher had joked that there was nothing more silent and reverent than a group of people with food in front of them.

After lunch, John became a silent observer as the team discussed budget, construction bidding, zoning, permitting and all the fine details involved in the development. These discussions went on for several hours. Once concluded, Dennis asked for a motion to approve the master plan. A motion was made and seconded, and a unanimous vote approved the plan. Dennis tasked two of the team members to prepare a presentation for the zoning board and to draft the documents for building permits. He turned to John.

"John," he said, "We greatly appreciate your work creating this master plan. You have done a spectacular job of designing a beautiful work/live community that I believe will be a great success. The teams will be in touch if they need any support for their preparation for zoning and permitting."

John stood and shook his hand. "It is always a pleasure to work with your firm. If I can assist in any way moving forward, feel free to contact me."

Dennis walked him to the receptionist area just outside the conference room and asked the girl at the counter to call John's car service. The two shook hands again and Dennis returned to the conference room. John retrieved his suitcase from the receptionist and headed to the lobby where he found a comfortable sofa to wait for the car service. Within a few minutes, a black town car pulled up in the circular driveway and to the glass doors. John stood up and grabbed his suitcase and rolled it behind him as he walked out the glass doors.

"John," said the driver as he opened the rear car door; "my name is Miguel. I understand you are staying at the Hyatt. Is that correct?"

119

"Yes Sir," John said.

"Excellent," Miguel replied.

John slid into the back seat as Miguel stored his suitcase in the trunk. Miguel crawled in to the driver's seat and turned to John.

"Would you like me to drive you to a local restaurant for dinner?"

"That would be nice, but I hate to be an inconvenience," John replied.

"No inconvenience at all, Sir," Miguel said. "I am at your service. What are you hungry for?"

John thought for a moment and then responded with a knowing grin, "Barbeque."

Miguel flashed a wide smile, "I know just the place for you!"

Within a few minutes, Miguel pulled up in front of a large adobe building with an old covered wagon out front and an array of cacti surrounding the building. When he opened the door for John, he could instantly smell the aroma of meat cooking over mesquite wood.

"Oh that smells divine," John said as he stepped out of the car.

"The food taste even better than it smells," Miguel noted. "Take your time and enjoy your dinner. I will be waiting just past that sign," he said, pointing to a section of the parking lot.

"Thank you, Miguel," John said and headed to the front door of the restaurant.

He was quickly seated at a corner table and a waitress took his drink order. Within a matter of minutes she returned with a Lone Star beer and a bucket of parched peanuts. John ordered a beef brisket dinner and sipped his beer. He retrieved his phone and texted his wife, "Meeting went well. The plan was unanimously approved, and they are headed to zoning and permitting.

I'm sitting in a barbeque joint enjoying a Lone Star and waiting for brisket. I love you."

Moments later, his phone buzzed. He looked down at a text message in reply, "John! How could you! Having brisket without me? I am wounded to the core. LOL I love you too. Eat some for me."

He laughed at the response and emptied the beer. Before he had the bottle back on the table, the waitress arrived with another. Just a few minutes later, she returned with a huge platter of succulent meat, baked beans mixed with bacon and ground beef, corn on the cob, and coleslaw.

"Now THAT is what I'm talking about," John said as she sat the platter down in front of him. John savored every bite of the meal until there was nothing remaining on the plate, taking the last piece of Texas toast and mopping the platter clean. When the waitress returned and saw the empty platter, she joked.

"I guess you didn't like it," she said with a giggle.

John held up the end of the platter, "I cleaned it so well, you don't even need to send it to the dishwasher. You can just put this platter back in the cabinet," he joked.

"How about a bowl of hot blackberry cobbler for dessert?"

John blew out his cheeks, "I couldn't eat another bite unfortunately," he said, somewhat disappointed at turning down cobbler.

She smiled and handed him the check. He stuck a credit card in the book holding the check and finished off the remaining Lone Star while she closed his check. When she returned, he totaled out the check, put the receipt in his wallet, stood up and headed for the door. Once outside, he spotted the town car right where Miguel said he would be. As he approached the car, Miguel popped out and opened the rear door for him.

"Well," he said, "How did I do on the recommendation?"

John patted him on the shoulder. "That, he said, "was amazing."

"I'm glad you liked it," Miguel replied with a smile.

Miguel drove him to the hotel and stopped in front of the door to the lobby. John tipped him and Miguel handed him a business card.

"When you come downstairs for breakfast in the morning, call me," he said. "And when you have eaten, I will be here ready to take you to the airport."

"Sounds like a plan," John said.

Miguel retrieved his bag for him and rolled it to the lobby door.

"Have a good night's rest," Miguel said.

"Thanks Miguel," John replied, "You too."

John walked into the hotel lobby as Miguel drove off into the night.

Chapter 23

Phil awoke to the alarm on his phone. He shut it off and sat up, looking at the other bed, noticing that it was vacant and made as if a maid service had visited. He turned his head toward the front of the Airstream to see Sam fully dressed sitting in the swivel chair drinking coffee reading his Bible. Phil shook his head. He got out of bed and headed for the shower. He completed his morning ritual and dressed for the day. He returned to the bedroom area and finished repacking his suitcase. Following Sam's lead, he made the bed. Then he walked to the front of the trailer and poured himself a cup of coffee in a paper cup.

"Are you ready to head to the airport?" Phil asked Sam.

Sam looked up over his glasses, "I don't know if I ever want to leave here," Sam quickly replied.

"Understood," Phil responded. He opened the trailer door and put Sam's suitcase just outside the door, then retrieved his own and carried it out. He loaded both the suitcases in to the back of the SUV, then he headed back into the Airstream for his laptop and his cup of coffee. Sam pushed himself up out of the chair with the aid of the cane and carefully descended the two folding steps from the trailer to the ground.

They climbed into the SUV and Phil cranked the motor. They both took one look around as Phil pulled the shifter in drive and headed out to Hog Eye Road. They snaked along a couple of roads until they reached Farm to Market Road and eventually ended up on Texas Highway 71, just outside the front gate to the airport. Phil followed the signs to the rental car return and stopped in a line of returned cars where a young man in a vest waved him over. While the young man scanned the tag on the windshield and checked the fuel and mileage, Phil retrieved their suitcases from the back and tossed his laptop bag over his shoulder. The young man printed Phil's receipt from a handheld device and handed it to him. Phil thanked him and walked around to the passenger side where Sam was slowly exiting the vehicle.

"You look exhausted," Phil noted.

"Well," Sam began, "it has been a big week."

Once inside the terminal, Phil requested a roller chair for Sam. A red cap quickly appeared and helped Sam get seated. They then headed for the security line. Security moved Sam through quickly, while Phil went through the normal slower process. Once cleared, Phil stopped to put on his belt and shoes and repack his laptop.

"Alright, Sam," he said, "let's get to the coffee."

Sam grinned. They rolled up to a kiosk, Phil bought them both a large cup of coffee and then followed the red cap pushing Sam to the gate. The red cap wheeled the roller chair to a row of seats at the gate directly in front of the gate agent podium. Sam used his cane to help push himself up to a standing position. He thanked the red cap and shook his hand. Phil walked behind him and as Sam sat down in one of the padded chairs at the gate, Phil palmed the red cap a twenty dollar bill. He then returned to where Sam was seated, handed him his coffee, and then sat down in the seat next to him. Phil's phone vibrated, so he pulled it out of his pocket and pushed a button. He shook his head as he read the screen of his phone.

"Well Sam, this flight has been cancelled, and they have moved us to another flight scheduled to depart 20 minutes later than our original," he said.

"Well 20 minutes isn't too bad I guess," Sam said staying positive.

"We are going to have to walk to another gate," Phil added. "Fortunately it is just three gates down."

He stood and pulled his laptop bag over his shoulder. Sam slowly stood up using the cane for leverage.

"I'll pull my bag," Sam said. "You have your hands full with a coffee and a suitcase."

Phil nodded, and tugged his bag over onto its wheels. Sam shoved the cane under his arm so he could carry coffee in one hand and pull his bag with the other. They slowly walked to the new gate assignment and found two seats near the gate agent podium just like they had selected at the prior gate. They quietly finished their coffees and divided their attention between people watching and the news on the overhead televisions.

Within an hour, the gate area became flush with passengers. Sam looked around and wondered how they would all fit on the plane. He was a bit anxious having heard stories of airlines bumping passengers off flights and the thought of sitting in an airport for hours on end. A gate agent walked up to the podium and began typing on a keyboard to a computer. After a few minutes, she began calling passengers to the podium and handing them boarding passes. Sam and Phil were the last two names she called. They both received their new boarding passes and sat down together reviewing them.

"Well," Phil noted, "Looks like we aren't sitting together, but the good news is that we are still in the first class section."

When boarding began, Sam boarded early to allow him the extra time he needed to walk the jetway at his regular pace. A flight attendant stowed his bag in the overhead bin above his seat, and Sam slid into the window seat on his row. After several more minutes, the remaining first class passengers began to board. A tall dark haired bearded man stopped at the seat beside him and hoisted his bag into the overhead bin. He pulled a laptop bag off of his shoulder and pushed it under the seat. He sat down in the seat next to Sam.

"Good morning," he said.

"Good morning", Sam replied.

The man stuck out his hand. "I'm John," he said. "What's your name?"

Sam shook his hand, "I'm Sam."

"Nice to meet you Sam," the man replied. "Are you from Atlanta?"

"As a matter of fact I am," Sam answered; "Born and raised."

"Me too," John replied, "What brings you to Austin?"

Sam reached into his sports coat pocket and pulled out a pamphlet. "Well, I pastor a church in downtown Atlanta and we have been discovering the overwhelming homelessness around our area. We heard about this village just outside of Austin, so we came to take a look at what they were doing and see if we could learn a little something," Sam explained.

John took the pamphlet and began browsing it. John was stunned and silent for several minutes as he read about a master planned community tailored to the needs of the homeless population in the Austin area. He could not believe his eyes. Finally after a few minutes, he was able to overcome the rush of emotions he felt bursting inside him.

"Sam," he said, "You are not going to believe this but I design master planned communities for a living. In fact, I came to Austin to deliver the final design to a developer here for a master planned live work community on the north side just outside of Round Rock."

Sam snatched his head to look John in the eyes. "You're kidding me," he said.

"Actually," John continued, "I'm as serious as a heart attack. And if that doesn't shock you this next bit of information I am about to share just might."

"Try me," Sam responded.

"Well," John continued, "My uncle passed away several months ago and left me a large tract of land down near the Atlanta Motor Speedway and a section of it contains a mobile home park. It's over an hour's drive from our house, and I have been struggling to try and manage it."

"Wow," Sam replied and reached down and pinched his own thigh. He squirmed from his own pinch. "I guess I'm not dreaming, because that certainly hurt."

John laughed, "My wife and I have been talking about trying to find a church or group to donate the mobile home tract. If you started something like this village," he said referring to the pamphlet, "you could have probably 10 people living on the property within a matter of days before even drafting a master plan."

Sam's eyes grew wide, "You said you were entertaining the idea of donating the tract with the mobile home park?"

John laughed again, "Yeah. So this is quite the opportune meeting I would say," he said.

"Yes. Yes it is," Sam replied. "A divine appointment I believe."

Through the remainder of the boarding process, take off and flight, the two continued to talk. Sam relayed the story of Peachtree Church's current operation status, the events during the winter storm, and his impending retirement. The more John listened, the more he was encouraged to support the idea of designing and creating a community outside of Atlanta that those struggling with homelessness could call home. When the flight landed in Atlanta, Sam knew he needed to connect John and Phil. He looked around the first class cabin to locate him. Finally he saw him four rows ahead of him on the other side of the aircraft.

"John, I want to introduce you to the president of the board of our church who came out here with me to see the village outside of Austin. Any chance you would have a few minutes when we get off for a quick introduction?"

"I'll do you one better than that," John replied, "Why don't we sit down and have lunch at one of the restaurants together here in the airport?"

Sam was surprised by the offer. "Well I don't want to be an imposition. I am sure you have places to be and things to do," he said.

John smiled. "I am going to need to eat lunch anyway, why not make it productive?"

When the plane landed, it took several minutes for the pilot to taxi across the myriad of taxiways at the huge Atlanta airport and finally pull up to the assigned gate. Sam hardly heard the flight attendant or the captain's announcements. Once the aircraft door was open, Phil quickly appeared in the aisle next to Sam's row to help with his suitcase.

"Phil," Sam said," I want to introduce you to John. He designs master planned communities."

Phil was stunned for a moment as he thought to himself, "What are the chances?" He quickly gathered his composure and shook John's hand.

"Pleasure to meet you," Phil greeted him.

As the three began their walk up the jetway, Sam gave Phil his second surprise of the day. "John has invited us to lunch to discuss the possibilities of launching a master planned community for the homeless outside of Atlanta."

Phil quickly glanced at John. "Seriously?" Phil asked, in a bit of shock.

John chuckled. "As serious as a heart attack, Sir. I even have a piece of land I can donate to get it started," he said with a wide grin.

Phil smiled, "well then, lunch is on me."

"Oh no," John responded, "I can write it off as a business expense. You're not stealing my tax write-offs," he joked.

John led the three to a restaurant on the concourse that had sit-down service on the second level, providing a quieter place to talk. A young waiter took their orders and John began the conversation. "Sam has told me a bit about your experiences over the last couple of weeks and what you just observed in Austin, and it sounds like you would like to do something similar in Atlanta."

Phil nodded in agreement. "Yes, Sir," he said. "Over the last few days, I have been working on the paperwork we need to launch an independent nonprofit completely separate from Peachtree Street Church. I believe this will allow us to acquire grants, corporate sponsorship, as well as support from other churches regardless of denomination. I have made a list of business leaders in the area that I have relationships with that could possibly serve on the board. And, I have been drafting the vision and mission statements so we have something to begin massaging once we have a formal board."

It was Sam's turn to be shocked at this point. "Is that what you have been working on during this whole trip?".

"As a matter of fact it is," Phil said with a smile, "I figure we need something established before you retire."

Sam smiled. "I guess we do," he said.

After the waiter had delivered the food, Sam said a prayer and the men began eating.

John continued, "Well as it happens. I have several acres near the Atlanta Motor Speedway in an unincorporated area that I inherited from my late Uncle. It has become more than I can keep up with and frankly, it's wearing me out. There is a mobile home park on the land that we are beginning the process of closing down. The mobile home park has five trailers on it that we own that are in pretty good shape. Each one is a two bedroom, so theoretically, you could put ten people on the property day one."

Phil looked at Sam. "I think I need to pinch myself."

Sam chuckled. "Don't," he said; "I already did and it hurts like the dickens."

Phil laughed.

John handed both of the men his business card. "Here is my card," he said, "I like this idea so much I'm going to make you an offer. One - My family will donate the mobile home park to your organization once you have inspected it and determine it is up to your requirements. Two - I will provide the organization first right of refusal on the remainder of the land. Three - I will design the master plan for developing the entire property to the organizations requirements pro bono. And, four - at some point, I would like to be considered for the board of directors. You do not have to respond to this four-part offer immediately. Let's set up a time to ride out and look at the property, and you can see what you think. I will send you a copy of my portfolio, so you can see what kind of work I have done in the past for other clients. Y'all can consider all of the offer, and we can get back together in a few weeks to see how you would like to proceed."

When he concluded his statement, he noticed both men had stopped eating. Phil looked at Sam and Sam looked back at Phil. Almost simultaneously as if choreographed, the two men looked back at John.

"Are you sure you want to engage this far this early?" Phil asked. "That is an awfully big leap of faith for partnering with two guys you just met on a plane"

John chuckled, "Guys, I'll be honest with you. This sounds like the best use of that land I have ever imagined. And with the enormity of the homeless population in Atlanta, I cannot think of a better cause to get behind."

The men continued to chat until they had all finished their lunch. The waiter returned with the check and John quickly grabbed it and placed his American Express card in the book and closed it.

"I was serious when I said I was expensing this as a business luncheon with a potential client," he said and handed it to the waiter.

"Well thank you," Sam said. "Thank you for lunch. And thank you for this generous offer."

"Yes, Thank you," Phil said. "Check your calendar once you get back into your office and let us know a good time to tour the property."

"Sounds like a plan," John replied.

The waiter returned with the check, John completed it, signed a copy, and tucked the other copy in his laptop bag.

"Well, if you gentlemen will excuse me," he said, "I am sure my wife and kids would like to see me before dinner."

"Absolutely," Sam replied.

They stood up, shook John's hand and thanked him again. The three started for the escalator to the transportation level. Sam and Phil fell behind John's quick pace, and he was quickly out of sight. The two men boarded the airport train. Sam found a seat in one end of the train and sat down. Phil stood in front of him holding onto an aluminum pole. After several stops, they reached the stop for the main terminal and exited the train and stepped onto the tallest escalator that Sam believed he had ever encountered. After a few minutes, they ascended into the bustling main terminal near the baggage claim. Phil led Sam to the exit directly across from the parking deck. Sam was beginning to tire from the walk and his pace showed it.

Once outside the terminal, they stopped at the curb for a break in traffic to cross the airport road to the parking deck. When they stopped, Phil noticed a heavy sigh from Sam.

"You OK there Sam?" Phil asked.

"Yeah. It's been a long week," Sam replied.

Phil spotted a break in the seemingly endless line of traffic, and they began to cross. He led them up a ramp where he stopped in front of a vending machine and paid for his parking. He then led them to an elevator that took them to the floor where Phil's Mercedes was parked. A little more walking and they reached Phil's car. Phil opened the passenger side door for Sam and helped him get seated and then stowed their luggage in the trunk. Phil opened the driver's door and slid into the driver's seat.

"If you like," Phil said, "that seat reclines with the button there on the door rest."

Sam looked at the armrest on the door and located a button. He reclined the seat a bit and settled in for the drive back into Atlanta. Phil wound his way out of the parking deck and to one of the many exit gates. He stopped in front of a kiosk screen at one of the booths and inserted the ticket he had received at the vending machine where he had paid for parking. The kiosk opened the gate and printed out a parking receipt. Phil took the receipt, rolled up his window, and drove out of the gate onto the busy airport road. A couple of lane changes and Phil had the car pointed North on I-85. He turned to check on Sam and noticed that he was asleep.

Chapter 24

Sam woke up several times during the night and in the early hours of Friday morning not because he was in pain - no more than normal anyhow. Nor was he wakened by a fitful bladder or things that rattle garbage cans and window shutters. He was waking up thinking about the homeless men, women, and children he had encountered during the winter storm and those he had met outside of Austin who now had homes. He marveled at the difference in the quality of life and the glimmer of hope and light that he saw restored in those eyes. Finally, he could not bear tossing and turning over anymore, so he got up, heated a kettle of water on the stove, and brewed himself a cup of hot tea. He sat down in his chair in the living room area and picked up the book he had bought while in Austin. He sat motionless and silent reading and sipping his tea, stopping only for a moment to wipe a tear from his eyes, then he resumed turning pages. When he finished the book, he looked up at the clock on the wall and realized he had been reading for two and a half hours. He stretched his tired joints and carried his mug back to the kitchen and sat it on the counter. He turned back to the bedroom and began his morning routine and dressed for his day.

When he walked back out of the bedroom, his cell phone was ringing. He unplugged it from the charger, flipped it open and answered it.

"Hello?"

"Good Morning, Sam," said the voice, "It's Phil. Are you about ready to ride down and take a look at John's property?"

"Absolutely," Sam replied, "I couldn't sleep from the anticipation. Hurry over here and let's get moving."

Phil chuckled, "I don't recall you ever being in much of a hurry, Sam."

"Well now you've seen it," Sam replied with a laugh.

"I hope it is alright with you," Phil continued, "I have invited a couple guests to join us."

"Oh?" said Sam.

"Yeah," Phil replied, "I talked to a couple guys in my circles who I thought might be interested in corporate sponsorship and asked them if they would like to join us for the first look."

Sam smiled, "That sounds great."

"OK," Phil said, "We will see you in a few minutes."

Sam wondered who Phil might have with him while he waited for his arrival. He knew Phil moved in some pretty influential circles, so it made it hard for him to narrow it down to one or two community leaders. He walked over to the window and opened the blinds so he could look out on the parking lot. Shortly he saw the lights of the Mercedes turn in to the parking lot. He grabbed his cane and scurried for the door. He walked out of the door to the apartment and locked the door behind him and then scurried down the steps the best he could. As Phil was stepping out of the car, he saw Sam approaching.

"Slow down there Tiger," he exclaimed. "We don't need you taking a tumble."

"Thanks for the concern," Sam responded; "I'm alright."

The passenger door of the Mercedes opened and out stepped a man in a suit. The rear door of the Mercedes opened and out stepped another man that Sam swore he recognized but could not quite place him. The first man approached him with an outstretched hand.

"Reverend Matthews," he said, "It is nice to meet you. I'm Roger Phillips."

Sam shook his hand. "Nice to meet you Roger. You can call me Sam."

"Roger heads up community involvement with a large building supply corporation headquartered here in Atlanta," Phil noted.

The second man approached Sam and greeted him with an outstretched hand as well.

"Reverend Matthews, I'm Bill Hammond," he said, "I'm Vice President for a national fast food franchise group headquartered here in town."

Sam shook his hand. "Nice to meet you as well, Bill."

Roger looked at Sam. "Sam, why don't you ride up front here? I'll ride in the back with Bill."

Phil escorted Sam over to the passenger side and helped him into the car. They all buckled in and Phil started the car, put it in gear, and started out of the parking lot. He paused momentarily at the exit onto the street and pushed some selection on the screen in the middle of the dash.

"I've got the address entered here, so we can use navigation to get us there," he explained.

"So fellas, I understand that you looked at a large master planned community in Texas for the homeless," said Roger. "What kind of housing did they utilize?"

Phil quickly began explaining, "They had a variety of housing elements in the village - travel trailers, recreation vehicles, and tiny homes. I don't know how much you gentlemen have been exposed to the tiny home movement, but there is quite a variety of homes under 500 square feet that are becoming very popular these days. Some of the ones we saw had large wrap around porches while others were two story loft arrangements. The builders were quite creative in maximizing every inch of space and leveraging outdoor space as well."

Roger nodded his head. "Yes. We have seen a lot of development across the country in the tiny home segment from construction on 8x12 trailer frames, railroad caboose renovations, and storage container based homes. It seems to be a booming trend in the starter home segment," he noted.

Sam chimed in, "They are economical solutions that really fit the need for providing a home to someone who has been without. It is certainly a step up over sleeping in a doorway, under a bridge or even in a tent. Tiny homes provide a restoration of privacy and self-sufficiency. Several of the people we talked to were ecstatic to be provided a 12-foot travel trailer with a clean bathroom, a dry mattress, and a working stove and refrigerator. We tend to take a lot of things for granted until you sit and talk with someone that has been struggling with survival while homeless."

"If you had available utilities and basic infrastructure, a tiny house could be built between $10,000 and $15,000," Roger said, "So theoretically a $100,000 grant or corporate sponsorship could provide 10 homes."

"Those are the numbers I have been working," Phil commented, "I figure we could completely furnish an 8' x 12' home for just under $15,000."

Bill had been listening attentively to the conversation. "You show any corporation in the Atlanta metro area that you can provide a proper home to someone for $15,000, and I think you will be pleasantly surprised how many would be willing to sponsor a couple of homes," he said. "And you know, we both have friends that work for other corporations in the area. So if we get involved, we are going to tell a couple of friends and they get their companies involved. The next think you know, you have a considerable level of corporate support."

"That is my hope," Phil responded. "It may seem a like a bit of conflict of interest at first, but the gentleman who is going to show us this land designs master planned communities. He has offered to donate a tract of this land that has a working mobile home park on it as well as his services to design a master planned community on the remaining land."

"That is a pretty significant donation," Roger said. "The design work alone can run in the six figures. Then you figure in the value of the land donation on top of that - it certainly isn't an offer to take lightly."

"Has he mentioned his asking price on the remaining land?" Bill asked.

"No he hasn't at this juncture," Phil responded. "Just that we would have the right of first refusal on it."

"So where are you on organizational development?" Bill asked.

"I have drafted the vision, purpose, and articles of incorporation. And I have started drafting the application for 501c3 nonprofit status for the IRS." Phil replied.

"Excellent," Bill said, "It is kind of exciting to be given the opportunity to become involved at the ground level."

Phil had purposely avoided the interstate option and chosen to take highway 41 instead. He had seen all of the interstate congestion he could possibly want for a while. They passed the main entrance to the Atlanta Motor Speedway and after a couple more miles turned onto a two-lane road. At first the road led them between subdivisions, but after a while they gave way to single homes on a few acres of land. Then they began to see livestock and barns on bigger expanses of land. As the road curved around, they could see the outline of the grandstands for the race track off in the distance while both sides of the road were dotted with pine trees and pastures. Finally they arrived at the entrance to a mobile home park. It was neatly mowed and seemed well kept. There were several empty lots and five homes sitting on adjacent lots. All of the homes were freshly painted and neat in appearance.

Phil pulled up next to a pickup truck and parked the car. He shut the car off, and they all began to get out and look around them. The nearest trailer had an office sign next to it. The door to that trailer swung open, and John stepped out to greet them.

"Good Morning, Gentlemen," he said with a smile.

He walked across a small deck and down the steps to where they were standing.

Phil introduced him to Bill and Roger.

"So this mobile home park consists of 25 acres and has 60 pads on it that can support single or doublewide trailers. These 5 homes in front of you belong with the property and are two bedroom units. You would be free to place mobile homes, RVs or even tiny homes on the remaining 55 lots. There is county water at each pad and the park has its own private septic system. The park has underground utilities, so you will notice a panel and meter base at each pad. As I mentioned before, if you choose to accept the mobile home park as a donation, you could house 10 people right off the bat while you conduct fundraising to build out the other 55. When you fill this up, our family has an adjoining 200 acres that we would be willing to provide you first right of refusal," John said.

Sam looked at the other three men standing beside him. "I cannot see any reason why we wouldn't accept the offer," he said.

Phil smiled. "Can we take a look inside the trailers?"

"Sure," John answered. "Three still have renters living in them, but they have been provided notice that we are closing business. So they are in the process of relocating, but are happy to let you see the inside of their units. Why don't we start here with the office unit? The manager has lived here and managed the property from the living room. He has already vacated, so it's clean and empty."

The men walked through the mobile home and were pleasantly surprised by how clean it was. Every room looked spotless as if it were a brand new home. They toured the other four units and then returned to the deck of the office unit.

"What kind of zoning regulations do you have to contend with here?" Phil inquired.

"The county has the basic building permit process, but it isn't anything like inside the city. As you probably noticed on the way in, this is still a pretty rural agricultural area. This tract is surrounded by my family's land, so you will not have issues with neighbors complaining. There has been a mobile home park here for 30 years," John replied.

Roger looked at Phil. "I am pretty sure I could get you a grant to build ten homes here once you have your 501C3," he said.

Phil and Sam smiled at each other.

Bill chimed in, "I will personally donate enough to build two and get our company to fund another ten."

Sam looked at Phil. "I guess we need to get busy."

John stood to one side of the deck watching the conversation take place. "Am I to take it that this meets your inspection?"

Phil stepped towards him. "Yes, Sir. It certainly does." He shook John's hand. "Thank you for this generous offer."

John smiled. "My family is happy to support this cause. I will contact my attorney's office and have them draft closing documents. Call me when you have your articles of incorporation filed, and we will schedule the closing."

Every one of the men shook John's hand and thanked him. They walked around the park for several minutes before returning to Phil's car.

Chapter 25

Lewis' cell phone rang. It caught him by surprise, as he did not get many calls. He looked down at the caller ID display before flipping it open to answer it. The number did not seem familiar to him, but he decided to answer the call anyhow.

"Hello," he said with his forehead wrinkled, wondering who was calling.

"Lewis," the voice on the other end said, "This is Reverend Samuel Matthews. We met at the hospital waiting room when Miss Gladys was having surgery after the storm."

"Oh Yeah," Lewis replied; "How are you doing Reverend?"

"I am doing pretty good, Lewis," Sam replied. "I was wondering if you would be interested in a project we have started."

"What sort of project would that be?"

"Well," Sam continued, "I want to offer you your own home. A group of us have acquired some land several miles outside of town. We have a couple furnished mobile homes that we are giving to a few deserving souls. And you came to the top of my mind. We are trying to create a community that looks out for one another. After seeing how you came looking to see about Miss Gladys, I thought this would be a perfect opportunity for you."

Lewis was stunned. He did not know what to say or how to react. Was this real? Could this really be happening?

"What's the catch?" Lewis asked intently.

"What do you mean?" Sam asked in response.

"What do I have to do?"

"You don't have to do anything Lewis," Sam explained. "This is a no strings arrangement. If you want to accept it, you will become the owner of a fully furnished two-bedroom mobile home. If you decide that you would like to share your home, you are welcome to offer the second bedroom to anyone of your choosing. You do not have to make a decision this minute. But if you are interested, I would be more than happy to drive you out to see the home, and let you see what you think."

"Well, I don't have anything on my calendar for the next..." Lewis stopped himself mid sentence. "I have no plans. I guess I could go see it with you whenever you like."

"Alright then," Sam said, "When could you meet me in front of the Chick-Fil-a at Colony Square?"

"In about 15 minutes," Lewis replied.

"OK. I'll meet you there. We can grab a couple of lunches and drive out to see the home," Sam suggested.

"Alright. I'm headed that way," Lewis said and closed his phone. He started walking the 6 or so blocks towards Chick-Fil-A. When Sam rounded the corner, he saw an old ex-cop car sitting in the circular driveway right in front of a "No Parking" sign.

"Reverend Matthews," Lewis said as he approached the driver's window.

"Hello Lewis," Sam replied.

"Reverend Matthews, these folks are bad about booting cars around here, so you better stay with your car. I'll go inside and see what I have left on my gift card," Lewis suggested.

"No Sir," Sam sternly responded. "I'll stay with the car, but you take this $20 bill. Lunch is on me."

Lewis started to protest, but Sam already had his hand up, "I won't hear it, Lewis," he said.

"Alright, alright. But can I get you something?" Lewis relented.

"Sure, just a sandwich and a sweet tea, since they dropped the coleslaw I loved so much from their menu. I sure don't want a kale salad," Sam replied.

Lewis laughed, "Alright. You sit tight."

"Why don't you put that big back pack in the back seat. I'll keep an eye on it for you," Sam suggested.

Lewis smiled, "You know, I didn't even think about that. I'm so used to having to guard it and keep it with me all the time," he explained. "Pretty sure I can trust you with it," he added.

Lewis opened the rear car door and laid the backpack on the backseat. He then disappeared down the stairs towards the front doors. After several minutes, he popped up carrying a paper bag and two drinks. He walked over to Sam's window and handed him a drink. He then walked around to the other side and crawled in the car and closed the door.

"Thank you for lunch," Lewis said. "Its kinda like Christmas - a free lunch and an offer of a free house."

Sam smiled, "You are more than welcome my friend."

Lewis handed Sam a foil wrapped sandwich.

Sam said, "Mind if I bless it?"

Lewis looked directly at Sam and then replied, "Not at all."

Sam prayed out loud, "Lord please bless this food and my brother Lewis. Bless our time together and help us bless those we meet. In Jesus name we pray, Amen."

Lewis emphatically said, "AMEN!"

Sam cranked the old tired Crown Vic and took a bite of his sandwich. "Let's go see your new home, Lewis," he said. While Sam drove, both men ate their sandwiches and savored the southern delight that is Chick-Fil-A sweet tea. After several minutes, Lewis polished off his sandwich and tossed the empty foil wrapper back in the paper bag.

"So Miss Gladys has been completing physical therapy in an extended stay wing of the hospital. When I saw her yesterday, they said they could release her. The social worker lady has been trying to get her to check into a shelter when she gets out," Lewis said.

"What's Gladys think about that idea?" Sam asked.

"Not a whole lot," Lewis replied, "She's not a big fan of the shelters."

Several miles later, they rounded the corner of the two-lane road and came up to the community. A metal archway stretched over the entrance that read "Homeland." Sam stopped the car and Lewis slowly looked around.

"It's a pretty far piece out of the city," he observed. "But this is quiet and peaceful."

Sam slowly began easing the car down the driveway towards the first trailer and pulled to a stop in front of the deck.

"What is that over there?" Lewis asked pointing off to the left of the driveway.

"Those are chicken coops," Sam explained, "There are laying hens in there that produce eggs. If you like, you can walk over there and get you a couple of eggs and make yourself breakfast or you can boil a couple for lunch."

Lewis nodded his head. "I do love a couple of eggs in the morning on the occasion I can get some," he said.

Sam smiled, "Here you can get some anytime you want."

Lewis squinted his eyes looking a little further down the driveway path. "Is that a garden over there?"

Sam shook his head, "Yes it is. There is sweet corn, green beans, tomatoes, squash, cucumbers ... all sorts of vegetables growing there, free for the picking."

Lewis paused in amazement. "Who keeps all this up? Who feeds the chickens and weeds the garden and such?"

Sam smiled. "Well, there is a fellow living in this first trailer here that was homeless. We met him during the storm. He stayed in our church for shelter that night. He loved to stay busy and work. We offered him this trailer, and he wanted to help manage things. So, he is the manager and a pretty good handyman."

The door to the trailer opened and out stepped Fred.

"Howdy Sam. Who ya have there with you this fine day?"

"Fred, this is Lewis," Sam said introducing him, "Lewis, meet Fred."

Hello, Fred," Lewis said, "I think I have seen you around before."

Fred nodded, "I believe you are right. I think we have seen each other on the streets of downtown. Thinking about joining us?"

"Thinking about it," Lewis admitted. "Kind of far to the free clinic or anything isn't it?"

"It is," Fred said, "but we have a Physician's Assistant that comes out twice a month to check on us, and he gets free samples of any medication that you have to have - takes pretty good care of us."

Lewis raised his eyebrows. "Well alright," he said.

Fred stepped off of the deck down to where Lewis and Sam were standing. "Lewis, let me show you the home that is available if you decide you want it," he said. "Walk this way."

He led Lewis over to the second trailer and unlocked the front door with a key on a ring hanging from his belt. Lewis stepped inside and could not believe his eyes. There was a comfortable looking recliner, a sofa, and a small television. He walked on in a little further and saw a wooden table and two chairs and a kitchen with a stove, refrigerator, microwave oven, a toaster, and even a coffee maker. His head was jerking from side to side trying to take it all in at one time.

"Walk on back past the kitchen," Fred suggested.

Lewis stepped into a hallway to see a washer and dryer. A few more steps and he could see a nice size bathroom with handles on the wall of the shower tub combo and another beside the toilet. He walked on down the hallway and stepped into a large bedroom with a bed that was made up with sheets and a comforter and two fluffy looking pillows. Lewis turned around and looked at Fred and Sam standing in the hallway.

"It all looks new," he noted.

"Because it is," Fred explained.

He looked at Sam.

"This is for me?" He asked, almost bewildered.

"If you want it," Sam responded, "it is yours for the asking."

"Heck there is another bedroom on the other side of the living room isn't there?" Lewis asked.

"There is," Fred answered, "With another full bathroom."

Lewis smiled and shook his head in disbelief.

"Preacher, you said I could pick a roommate if I wanted, right?" Lewis asked.

"That's right," Sam answered him.

"Would it be OK if we got the social worker lady to let Miss Gladys have that front bedroom? I don't want to upset church folks thinking we're shacking up or anything."

Sam smiled. "I think that would be fine, Lewis. She is going to need someone to help her get fully back up to speed. And I'm pretty sure we could get the local social services to help her right here."

Lewis nodded, "Well, if Miss Gladys can have the front bedroom. I'll take it."

Sam reached out to shake Lewis' hand, but saw tears rolling down his cheeks. He wrapped his arms around the big man and gave him a hug.

"Welcome home, Lewis," he said.

Fred walked up behind them and patted Lewis on the shoulder, "Welcome home, Lewis," he said.

Lewis wiped the tears from his cheeks and looked at Sam. "What do I have to do to move in?"

Sam chuckled. "Get your backpack out of my car and carry it into that back bedroom," he said.

Lewis looked up at him in disbelief.

"Really? I don't have to sign something or anything like that?"

"No," Sam answered him, "It is yours. It is a free gift."

Lewis walked over to Sam and gave him a huge bear hug while tears rolled down his cheeks.

"This is the most wonderful thing I have ever been given," he exclaimed.

Fred quietly walked out of Lewis' trailer and stopped at the edge of the deck that ran the length of the front of the trailer. He looked off in the distance and shook his head. A tear rolled down his cheek and then fell of his jaw. Fred never made an effort to wipe the tear away. He just kept shaking his head.

He looked up towards the sky and said, "This is good stuff right here, God. This is good stuff."

A few minutes the door to the trailer opened and Sam and Lewis stepped out onto the deck.

"There you are," Lewis said. "I wondered where you got off to."

Fred looked up at Lewis and shook his head.

"Just enjoying the air. It smells so sweet and clear here - so different than downtown," Fred replied.

Sam stepped near the two and said, "Guys. I would like to pray a blessing over Lewis' new house if that is alright with y'all."

Lewis nodded his head. "Sure," he said.

Sam bowed his head and began to pray. "Gracious Lord and Savior, thank you for all of the blessings you pour out on us each and every day. Thank you for these two men. Please bless Lewis and his new house. Let it be a blessing to him. May he be blessed coming and going, and may he bless everyone that he comes in contact with every day. We pray this in Jesus name, Amen."

"Amen!" Lewis and Fred said in unison.

"Were going to be getting more neighbors soon," Fred told Lewis. "We have three more trailers that I am finishing up the final touches on. Once those three are filled, we have 60 more spots that have all the utilities already run. We just need a tiny house, a mobile home, or a RV of some sort for those spots. There is a fella coming out tomorrow that will be putting up a large metal carport kind of structure that will be in the open area near my trailer. We have a large Barbeque grill and 10 wooden picnic tables that will go under it for a community area."

Lewis smiled. "You know I do love some good barbeque!"

He walked back to Sam's car and opened the back door and retrieved his backpack. He tossed it up on his shoulders and started back to his new home. He stopped at the door and turned to Sam and Fred.

"You know," he said; "This is going to be the first time I've ever unpacked."

Fred nodded his head. "Go slow," he recommended. "It is a lot to adjust to in one afternoon. Take it at your own pace. I was almost overwhelmed with it all when I first came out here. If you get bored during the day, you are more than welcome to hang out and talk to me while I work around here. But pace yourself; tonight will be the first time in a long time that you slept on a mattress with clean sheets and a brand new pillow. I'm hoping it's the best night of sleep you have ever had."

Lewis nodded as he listened to the advice.

"If you guys will excuse me. I think I am going to take a shower," Lewis said.

Fred nodded. "There are clean towels and washcloths under the sink in the two bathrooms. And if you open the top drawer on the chest of drawers in the bedroom, you will find new underwear and socks."

Lewis turned to Sam and Fred. "Thank you again. Thank you very much," he said.

He opened the door and walked into his new home. Closing the door behind him.

Sam looked at Fred with a smile. "You did pretty well for your first new resident," he said.

Fred grinned. "Thanks," he said, "I just kept thinking about what it was like when you and Phil brought me out here that day. It kind of helped me understand what he was feeling and thinking."

"Well," Sam started, "I think I am going to head back into town and try to catch up with Miss Gladys and her social worker and see if we can't get arrangements made to bring her out here if she is interested."

Fred shook his head. "I was really surprised that Lewis suggested that idea," he said.

"I wasn't," Sam replied, "Not for a minute. The second he said it, I thought 'That is the Lewis that I know.'"

"Have a good afternoon and drive safe," Fred said.

"You have a great afternoon and evening, Fred. Call me if you need me," Sam said.

Sam shuffled back to the tired old Crown Vic, cranked the motor and slowly drove toward the large archway entrance.

Fred stood motionless watching Sam drive off and out of sight. After a few minutes, he headed to trailer number three to assemble some furniture.

Chapter 26

Gladys was just polishing off the breakfast tray when the nurse knocked on her door.

"It's open," she responded, while finishing off the last fork full of grits and eggs.

The nurse walked to her bedside.

"Well are you ready for a road trip this morning?" the nurse asked, with a smile.

"Honey, nothing personal, but I am just ready to be out of this hospital," Gladys quickly answered.

"No offense taken, Miss Gladys. I completely understand. Are you sure you feel up to a long car ride?"

"Oh yeah," Gladys responded without a single thought, "I'm a tough old bird."

"OK," the nurse replied. "I have some discharge papers for you to sign. Miss Karen is out at the nurses' station. She will be in to see you in a minute. Let's get these papers signed and I will get you a wheel chair."

Gladys began signing the papers and continued the conversation as she signed. "I don't need a wheel chair. Y'all have had me up and down the hall with the walker and my funny looking cane."

The nurse smiled.

"Sorry Miss Gladys. Hospital policy due to insurance requirements. Anyone leaving the hospital goes to the front door in a wheelchair - even if they had a mole removed from their nose," she explained.

Gladys shook her head.

"Alright. I guess I won't win this fight, huh?" Gladys sighed.

The nurse looked over all the paperwork, tore out a couple duplicate pages and slid them in a binder.

"These are your copies. We recommend your see your surgeon for follow up. His office address and phone number are in this binder," she explained. "You weaned yourself off of prescription pain relievers. So if you have any pain, I would recommend taking an Aleve once every 24 hours as needed. Continue to walk and do the exercises the physical therapy staff taught you."

"OK," Gladys said, trying to patiently weather the sea of follow up information.

"I'm going to go get you a wheelchair now," the nurse said, and headed for the door.

As she stepped into the hallway, Gladys heard another voice.

"Miss Gladys?"

"Yes?"

Miss Karen walked in the room with a large smile on her face. "Well, look at you. Aren't you looking good today!"

Gladys laughed. "Kind of early in the morning to already be hitting the liquor isn't it, Miss Karen?"

Karen shook her head, "Gladys!" she laughed. "I came over in the mini-van, because I thought you might have a better time getting into it."

"Oh, OK," Gladys replied.

"Reverend Mathews and I have been talking and it sounds like they have a pretty nice home arranged for you. He wanted me to make sure you would be comfortable sharing the house with Lewis," Karen said.

Gladys nodded her head.

"Lewis is as harmless as a butterfly and has a heart of pure gold. He is kind of the male version of you Miss Karen," Gladys said.

"OK," Karen said, "I consider that a pretty good referral. Reverend Mathews is going to meet us at the home. Nothing is written in stone. If you don't like it and choose not to move in there, I can make arrangements for you in one of our shelters in town."

"Thank you, Miss Karen," Gladys responded. "I have always appreciated how you have looked out for me and the rest of the homeless community. Even though I haven't set foot in it yet, from what Reverend Matthews has told me I can't see myself not accepting the offer."

Karen smiled, "Alright. But just remember if anything changes, we can look at options for you. If you decide to move in there, they have arranged transportation so you can make your follow up appointments with the doctor. They also have a local social worker that checks in with the community there on a regular basis."

Gladys nodded her head. "Wonderful! I wondered how I would make that work."

The nurse appeared at the door to the room pushing a wheelchair.

"Are we ready to get rolling?"

"No pun intended I hope," Gladys said.

"I thought that was pretty clever," the nurse replied.

"Don't quit your day job," Gladys quipped.

Gladys slowly twisted herself sideways until her feet were hanging off the edge of the bed. She then began to push herself closer to the edge until her feet touched the floor and then lifted herself to standing.

"Couldn't have done that a week ago," she said proudly.

The nurse guided her into the wheelchair while Miss Karen collected her pack sitting by the edge of the bed.

"Miss Karen," said the nurse, "There is a large hospital bag just inside the wardrobe door there next to the bathroom too."

Karen walked over and opened the wardrobe door and picked up a large hospital bag.

"There's a couple of items the nursing staff bought as farewell gifts and a few toiletry items as well," the nurse noted.

The nurse began rolling Gladys down the hallway and toward the elevator while Karen followed behind carrying the bags. When they reached the elevator, the nurse pushed the down button and they waited. After several minutes, a down arrow above the elevator illuminated and a chime sounded. The doors to the elevator opened and the nurse wheeled Gladys inside and turned her around to face the door. Karen stepped inside and stood beside her.

When they reached the ground floor, the elevator doors opened and the nurse rolled Gladys a short distance to the exit doors. Karen went around them to the parking lot to get the van. She returned shortly and pulled to a stop right in front of where they were waiting. She walked around to the passenger side and opened the sliding door. Karen and the nurse helped Gladys getting into the van and getting seated. Karen loaded her walker and two bags in the back of the van while Gladys kept the three-legged cane by her side. Karen pushed a button on the key fob and the sliding door closed. She walked back around and climbed under the steering wheel.

She turned to Gladys. "Are you all buckled in and comfortable?"

"Oh yes," Gladys replied, "This seat is pretty comfortable."

"I tilted it a little to try and make you as comfortable as possible," Karen noted, "There are buttons on the door beside you that will let you adjust it however you like."

"Thank you, Miss Karen," Gladys said. "You are too kind."

Karen pressed some selections on the touch screen in the center of the dash and a navigation system began providing directions. Karen pulled the van into gear, and pulled out of the driveway and onto the street. She followed the directions up onto the Interstate and began travelling south.

After a few miles, Gladys struggled to keep her eyes open. Within a few minutes, she was asleep. Karen glanced in the rear view mirror. She smiled when she noticed that Gladys was napping during the ride.

When Gladys awoke, they were traveling down a small two-lane country road.

"Are we close?"

"As a matter of fact we are," Karen answered her.

They rounded a corner, and they could see the large metal arch over the entrance. Karen slowly drove down the driveway and pulled the van up to a large shelter. Smoke wafted from a grill cooking in the far end. She parked the van, pushed a button, and the door by Gladys slowly slid open. Karen retrieved the walker from the back of the van and carried it to the opened door.

"Miss Gladys, I think they have lunch ready for us!"

Gladys' eyes sparkled and danced. "I don't know what they are cooking, but it sure smells good to me!"

Karen helped Gladys out of the van. Gladys took the walker and began making her way to the shelter. She could see wooden picnic tables with balloons tied to the corners. She looked around and then looked at Karen.

"Miss Karen, is it somebody's birthday?" Gladys asked.

Before Karen could manage an answer, they heard a noise to their right. They turned to see Sam.

"Welcome to the Home Place, Miss Gladys," Sam said.

"Well thank you," Gladys said with a huge toothy smile. "Is it somebody's birthday?"

Sam chuckled. "No dear," he replied, "This is a welcoming party for you."

Gladys looked around her. "There must be a dozen people here," she thought. "Who are all these folks?"

Sam led her to a table that had a large cushioned chair at the end of it.

"We thought you would be a little more comfortable here than on one of the wooden benches," he said.

"Oh mercy! Thank you."

Sam helped her get seated and set the walker to one side of her.

"I want to introduce you to some people, Miss Gladys," Sam said.

He pointed to two men working at the grill. "I think you will recognize Lewis over there cooking. I'm not sure if you know him, but the other gentleman there is Fred. Fred lives here and serves as the Community Manager. Anything you need, you tell Fred, and he will take care of it."

He motioned to a group standing off to one side of him.

"These folks here are members of the board of directors for Home Place. They are responsible for making this dream a reality," Sam explained.

He introduced each board member to Gladys, and they each stepped to her and shook her hand.

"This gentleman's name is John. His family donated the land for Home Place, and he designed the master plan for the development of the community," Sam said.

John took his ball cap off and held it in his hand as he shook Miss Gladys's hand.

"It is a pleasure to meet you, Miss Gladys," John said. "I have heard a lot of great things about you from Sam and Lewis. I hope you enjoy the community."

Next Sam introduced Bill and Roger.

"Miss Gladys," he said, "these two gentlemen represent two corporations headquartered in Atlanta that are sponsoring the construction of 15 tiny houses that are being added to the community. Four are currently under construction, and we plan to have the rest completed by the end of the year."

"Wow!" Gladys exclaimed, "There are a lot of homeless in Atlanta that would love having a house here."

"We hope so," said Phil, who was now standing beside Sam. "We started with five mobile homes and by the end of this month those will all be fully occupied. So we are getting busy beginning the next phase. After lunch, I would like to show you around the property. Do you think you could stand a ride in a golf cart?"

"Oh, I imagine I could", Gladys replied. "I'm kind of anxious to see the rest of the beautiful place."

Lewis walked over to where they were with a plate in his hand.

"Miss Gladys. It sure is good to see you out and about," he said, almost tearing up.

"It's so good to see you Lewis," Gladys responded.

"Well I have a plate for you here. There's ribs, baked beans, tater salad, and coleslaw," he said setting the plate down on the table in front of her.

One of the board members brought her a solo cup filled with sweet iced tea and plastic utensils and napkins.

"There is banana pudding for desert," the lady said with a smile.

Gladys beamed with excitement. Everyone else lined up near the grill and began making up their plates. Sam and Karen came over and sat on either side of Gladys. Once everyone was served, Lewis and Fred brought over their plates and set down with them. Sam stood up.

"Thank you everyone for coming for this celebration. Let us pray," he said. "Father God, we thank you for the blessings of this day. Especially for this wonderful smelling food and the blessing of sweet iced tea. Thank you for Miss Gladys' continued healing and restoration. Thank you for everyone here and their dedication to providing homes to those who are homeless and a community where everyone feels welcome. In your son's holy name, Amen."

"AMEN," the group said in almost perfect unison.

When everyone finished their meals, Lewis and Fred began delivering small bowls filled with banana pudding. Gladys was amazed. She thought the food in the hospital had been pretty good - a huge improvement over some of the things she had eaten living on the streets of Atlanta. But this meal far surpassed anything she had eaten in years.

"Lewis," she shouted, "You never told me you could cook ribs that good. Man you ought to be running a restaurant!"

Fred fiercely nodded his head in agreement. "I've been telling him that for weeks now," he said.

When Gladys finished her lunch, Phil walked over to her.

"Miss Gladys are you ready for the fifty cent tour?" He asked jokingly.

"It depends," she replied, "Can I put it on my account? On account I don't have any money!" She laughed heartily at her own joke.

"That's a deal," Phil said.

Phil and Karen helped her up from the chair. She grabbed her walker and began shuffling alongside Phil as they walked over to a waiting golf cart. He helped her get seated and the put her walker in the back of the cart. They started slowly driving down the driveway.

"This is Fred's home and the community office," Phil said, pointing to the first trailer. "Right in front of it are the community mailboxes. Each one has a number corresponding to the house number."

They rode a little further.

"This is Lewis' home," he said pointing to the second trailer with a large deck running the full length of the front of the trailer. "And yours if you decide to accept it," he added.

"We will come back and walk through it in a minute," Phil said as he drove on slowly.

"This is the third house which will have two sisters moving in later this week. The fourth house has an Army Veteran and his best friend that will be moving in next week. The fifth house here has three candidates who have applied for it. The board will be making a selection this afternoon on who will be moving in there," Phil continued.

Just past the last trailer, Phil stopped the golf cart for a moment. Gladys looked up at a structure with four walls. The roof had not been built yet. Windows and doors had been framed out in the walls but were presently empty openings.

"This is going to be the community chapel," Phil announced, "It will only seat about 18-20 people. It's not necessarily designed to house Sunday morning services for the entire community. It is designed for a quiet place of reflection, meditation, and prayer."

Gladys smiled. "I bet Reverend Matthews is in love with this already."

Phil smiled and in a hushed voice asked, "Can you keep a secret?"

"Why yes." Gladys replied.

Phil whispered, "Sam doesn't know it yet. He thinks it's the next house. We have some amazing stained glass windows from an old country church that was torn down that will go in these window frames."

Gladys smiled. "He will absolutely love it!"

Phil pulled a little further down the drive, and Gladys could see signs in front of each lot. The signs displayed the name of the house that would be built there and had a listing of the sponsors responsible for funding the construction.

"These are the 15 tiny houses you spoke about earlier," Gladys remarked.

"Yes Ma'am," Phil said with a large smile.

"Are you ready to tour the home that Lewis is offering to you?" Phil asked.

"Absolutely!" Gladys answered quickly.

Phil turned the golf cart around in the driveway and started back to the second trailer. As they got closer, Gladys could see a couple of people playing horseshoes just to one side of the shelter where they had eaten lunch.

Phil stopped the golf cart at the edge of the deck. He stepped out of the golf cart and retrieved Gladys' walker. As he helped her to her feet, she stood up, grabbed the walker, and looked towards the trailer. Instantly she noticed three wooden steps leading to the front door. Before she could comment on the issues climbing steps with the walker, she noticed to her left there was also a ramp leading up onto the deck. As she began to make her way towards the ramp, she heard a couple of voices. She turned to one side to see Sam and Lewis approaching from the shelter.

With little assistance from Phil, Gladys made her way up the ramp with ease. Lewis hurried up the steps and across the deck to open the front door for her. Gladys crossed the deck and stepped into the living room and stopped dead still.

She slowly looked around her in wonderment. It was spotless. New furniture, a fully furnished kitchen, and clean as a whistle. Lewis walked in behind her and began to feed her the details of the floor plan and to her surprise he told her about the washer and dryer just down the hall way.

"Are you ready to see your room?"

"Yes, please," Gladys said softly.

Lewis pointed to a door at the end of the living room. Gladys shuffled her way to the door, opened it, and stepped into the bedroom. She stopped just inside the doorway looking at a queen size bed, dresser, chest of drawers, two night stands on either side of the bed, and in the corner a wing-backed chair. Lewis stepped in behind her.

"Over there," he said pointing to a door, "Is a full size bathroom with a shower that is handicap equipped. The door next to it is a walk-in closet."

Gladys stood stationary just looking around the room. Sam and Phil walked into the trailer and slowly walked to the bedroom door and watched Gladys' expressions.

"Well, Miss Gladys," Phil said, "What do you think?"

Gladys turned slowly towards him with tears rolling down both cheeks.

"I think this is the most wonderful gift I have ever received. I have wished and prayed for a dry place to sleep for years. I never dreamed of something this nice," she said, wiping at her cheeks and jaw line.

Lewis looked at her. "I would be honored if you would live here as my housemate," he said. "I will take care of the entire house including cooking and laundry until you feel like cooking and get tired of mine."

Gladys smiled and threw an arm in the air towards Lewis. He reached over and hugged her neck. The two smiled and cried. Karen walked in the trailer with Gladys' bags and set them down in the living room.

"Gladys," she said, "Can I help you unpack and move in?"

"Oh heaven's yes," Gladys replied.

Lewis stepped towards the bedroom door. "I will let you ladies tend to this. I better get back over and get things cleaned up from lunch."

"Seven out of 10 Americans are one paycheck away from being homeless."

Pras Michel

"Housing will never solve homelessness, but community will. It's not a transactional thing. It's a relational thing."
Alan Graham,
CEO and President,
Mobile Loaves and Fishes

"We want to make it socially, morally, politically and religiously unacceptable to have substandard housing and homelessness."
Millard Fuller

Epilogue

Just outside Austin Texas, sits a community called Community First! Village. It is a model for the world on how to address homelessness. Alan Graham, the founder of Community First! Village and Mobile Loaves and Fishes has done an amazing job of listening and addressing the needs of those struggling with homelessness. I highly encourage you to purchase and read his book, "Welcome Homeless - One Man's Journey of Discovering the Meaning of Home."

Appendix

The Point-in-Time (PIT) Count is an annual effort led by the U.S. Department of Housing and Urban Development (HUD) to estimate the number of Americans without safe, stable housing. Conducted annually in late January, HUD staff and volunteers attempt to count the number of homeless individuals on a single night across the United States. As one can imagine, locating and counting unsheltered homeless individuals is a daunting task and it is assumed the numbers are possibly low.

On a single night in January 2016, the Point-in-Time count identified 355,212 homeless nationwide of those 157,204 were unsheltered.

In the country's largest cities, the Point-in-Time count identified:

73,523 homeless in New York City, NY

43,854 homeless in Los Angeles City & County, CA

10,730 homeless in Seattle/King County, WA

8,669 homeless in San Diego City and County, CA

8,350 homeless in our nation's capital - District of Columbia

6,996 homeless in San Francisco, CA

6,524 homeless in San Jose/Santa Clara City & County, CA

6,240 homeless in Boston, MA

6,208 homeless in Las Vegas/Clark County, NV

6,112 homeless in Philadelphia, PA

5,889 homeless in Chicago, IL [i]

4,063 homeless in Atlanta, GA [ii]

Smaller cities also included in the report were Honolulu, HI with 2,797 homeless and St . Petersburg/Clearwater/ Largo/Pinellas County, FL with 2,383 homeless.

373,571 people (68%) were staying in emergency shelters, transitional housing programs, or safe havens, while 176,357 people were staying in unsheltered locations. There were 194,716 people in families with children experiencing homelessness, representing 35 percent of the homeless population. 330,890 people experiencing homelessness were men, while 217,268 people were women, and 1,770 people were transgender. Women experiencing homelessness were more likely to be sheltered than either men or transgender people. More than three-quarters of women experiencing homelessness 165,780 people were staying in emergency shelters, transitional housing programs, or safe havens, compared to 206,999 men, and 792 transgender people.

39,471 veterans were experiencing homelessness and there were 35,686 unaccompanied homeless youth.[iii]

These seem like staggering numbers, and one might find themselves asking how can one person make a difference. What could I do to change the tide of homelessness in my community? My suggestion is to begin by looking around your community. Does your community have a homeless population? Where are they? How many are there? What organizations are seeking to end homelessness? You can get a lot of answers to these types of questions by seeking out places to volunteer and serve in your community.

"Jesus comes to us in the poor, the sick, the dying, the prisoners, the lonely, the disabled, the rejected. There we meet him, and there the door to God's house is opened for us."

Henri Nouwen

Suggestions

- Sit down with a homeless person, buy them a meal, and ask them to share their story
- Own a rental property? Consider providing housing for a homeless family.
- Consider donating land or property to a homeless organization or leave an estate to them in a will.
- Encourage local leaders to address the issues causing homelessness instead of trying to sweep it out of sight.
- Buy a copy of Alan Graham's book, "Welcome Homeless - One Man's Journey of Discovering the Meaning of Home" and read it.
- Consider visiting Community First! Village and studying what they are doing with partnerships with corporations and private citizens.
- Consider starting a "Build-a-bed" program in your community. Bridgepoint Church in Saint Petersburg, Florida became aware of numerous children in their community that did not have beds. They began working with guidance counselors who identify children who are struggling in school and determine if they do not have a bed to sleep. Parents are then connected with the program and Build-A-Bed provides them a twin size bed, new mattress, sheets, a pillow, a stuffed animal, a night light, pajamas, a toothbrush and toiletries. The program began with two couples distributing beds one weekend a month. The program now delivers over 400 beds a year.
- Encourage your employer to sponsor a Habitat for Humanity home build.

Questions for Reflection

- How can I serve those in the community that can do nothing for me?
- Where can I volunteer that will bring me in contact with homeless in my community?
- Could I teach a trade or craft to a homeless person that they could use to become self-sufficient?
- What are my attitudes toward homeless people when I see them?
- Do I cast judgment on homeless people without knowing their story?
- What could I do for one, that I wish I could do for all?
- If I was homeless, what would I desire the most?
- What lengths would I go to if I learned my child was homeless and living on the street?
- What does God call me to do for those less fortunate than I am?
- How can I provide a hand up and not just a hand out?
- What could I change in my spending habits to allow me to financially support ending homelessness in my community?
- Who do I know that needs to read this book in order to stir their awareness of the plight of the homeless?
- Should my excess (income, time, and energies) be focused on me or on those around me?
- How can I be an advocate for the homeless in our community?

Other Books by Allen Madding

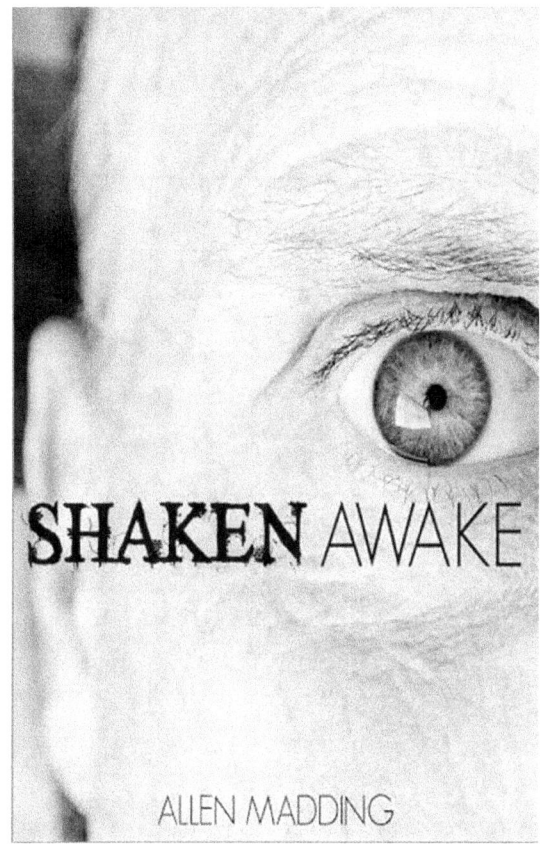

"Shaken Awake!" is the story of a church in downtown Atlanta, Georgia faced with a dwindling and aging congregation that has been forced to shut down the majority of their building and dismissed much of its staff. With limited funds, they shutter all of their ministries and programs leaving only a couple adult Sunday School classes and a Sunday morning worship service. When a homeless man freezes to death on the steps of their sanctuary, the church begins to re-examine their mission and priorities.

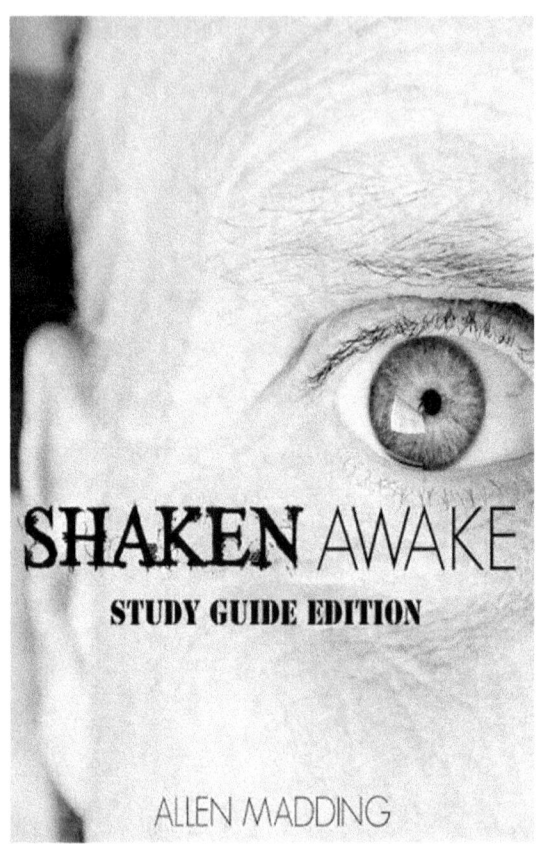

The **Study Guide Edition** breaks the story into a 5 week study - 3 short chapters of reading followed by questions to consider. Perfect for a book club or a small group study! It is the complete book and study guide combined in one easy to use paperback with room for writing your answers. 58 pages available in paperback only.

Available where ever quality books are sold and distributed by Ingram.

About the Author

Allen Madding is an advocate for families, children, the hungry and the homeless. He is a follower of the Way, writer, blogger, guitar player, hiker, traveler, car guy, Atlanta Braves and Dallas Cowboys fan, and an Information Technology professional who lives with his wife Allison in St. Petersburg, Florida.

Growing up in Mitchell county in rural South Georgia, he developed a love for hunting, fishing, and racing cars. He raced short track stock cars for nine years while operating a local computer store in his hometown and served as a volunteer fireman and EMT. He moved to Atlanta in 2000 taking a fulltime job in Information Technology management, and began writing weekly contributions for Speedway Media and then Insider Racing News.

After a short-term mission trip to Venezuela in 2011, he became keenly aware of the level of hunger in his community and began seeking a way to contribute. Allen and Allison launched Feed the Hungry Forsyth, Inc., a nonprofit food rescue organization in Cumming, Georgia, in December 2011 to collect unsold food from area restaurants and delivering to community food pantries. Together they have supported Habitat for Humanity participating in over 14 home builds, and they currently volunteer in the

Build-a-Bed ministry of Bridgepoint Community Church building and delivering beds to children who do not have their own beds.

[i] City of Chicago 2016 Homeless Point-in-Time Count & Survey Report (Prepared by the Voorhees Center for Neighborhood & Community Improvement, University of Illinois at Chicago)

[ii] 2016 Homeless Point in Time Count by Partners for Home

[iii] The 2016 Annual Homeless Assessment Report to Congress Part 1: Point-in-Time Estimates of Homelessness, The U.S. Department of Housing and Urban Development , Office Of Community Planning And Development, November 2016